The Road to Darkness

Translated from the German by
Mike Mitchell

Dedalus/Ariadne

Dedalus/Ariadne would like to thank The Austrian Ministry of Culture & Education in Vienna and The Eastern Arts Board in Cambridge for their assistance in producing this translation.

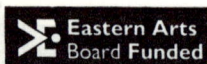

Published in the UK by Dedalus Ltd, Langford Lodge, St Judith's Lane, Sawtry, Cambs, PE17 5XE

UK ISBN 1 873982 33 X

Published in the USA by Ariadne Press, c/o Subterranean, P.O. Box 160, 265 5th Street, Monroe, Oregon 97456

US ISBN 1 5724 052 3

Distributed in Australia & New Zealand by Peribo Pty Ltd, 58 Beaumont Road, Mount Kuring-gai N.S.W. 2080

Distributed in Canada by Marginal Distribution, Unit 102, 277 George Street North, Peterborough, Ontario, KJ9 3G9

Daniel Jesus first published in 1905
Severin's Road to Darkness first published in 1914
The Ghost of the Jewish Ghetto first published in 1914/15
Texts copyright © Dierk O. Hoffmann
Translation copyright © Dedalus 1997

Typeset by RefineCatch Ltd, Bungay, Suffolk
Printed in Finland by Wsoy

A C.I.P. listing for this book is available on request.

THE AUTHOR

Paul Leppin was born in Prague in 1878 into an impoverished lower middle-class family. He worked until 1928 as a clerk in the Post and Telegram Service in Prague. His writing is rich in the sultry sexuality and morbidity of bohemian Prague typified by *Daniel Jesus* published in 1905. A member of the decadent literary cafe society he achieved notoriety with *Severin's Road to Darkness* in 1914, which marvellously captures the atmosphere of pre-World War 1 Prague.

Greatly influenced by Meyrink, he became a spokesman of the mysterious and the erotic atmosphere of old Prague, of which he became the 'Troubador'. He was arrested by the Gestapo in 1939 and suffered two strokes after his release and he died in 1945 from syphilis.

His last novel *Blaugast* written in 1932 and published post-humously in 1948 is featured in *The Dedalus Book of German Decadence*.

THE TRANSLATOR

Mike Mitchell is one of Dedalus's editorial directors and is responsible for Dedalus's translation programme.

His publications include *The Dedalus/Ariadne Book of Austrian Fantasy: the Meyrink Years 1890–1930*; *Harrap's German Grammar* and a study of Peter Hacks.

Mike Mitchell's translations include the Rosendorfer novels *The Architect of Ruins*, *Stephanie* and *Letters Back to Ancient China*, *The Works of Solitude* by Gyorgy Sebystyen and the novels of Gustav Meyrink.

CONTENTS

DANIEL JESUS

1

It was a long, aimless street down which Daniel Jesus was going in pursuit of an ugly evening. It kept in front of him; he could not catch up with it on his thin, aching legs which cast a hurried, flickering shadow on the wet cobblestones, irritating him and putting him in an ill temper. The evening ran before him like a mad, vicious animal, and he could not catch hold of it with his skinny fingers, could not grasp it by its tangled hair and stare long and hard into its dissolute eyes, feeling its hot breath streaming over his twitching eyelashes. For years his constant thought, his most intense yearning had been: If one could only strangle the evening! For evening was evil. Of course one had to be cautious, remain unobserved, approach it with simple, friendly words, smile and caress it as one would caress a woman. Oh, he would go about it cleverly! His hatred would glow inside him like an inspiration, helping him to find the right way to master the evening and kill it. He would abandon himself to it like a new-born babe, would be tender, passionate, lascivious. His eager hands would run over the flesh of that whore, making her sleepy, arousing her lust, until his fingers felt the black veins throbbing in her neck, hot with her lifeblood. Then they would close, suddenly, convulsively, pitilessly, and on her face the horrible expression would appear of which he dreamt every night. Oh God, why must he always think of it? But it was an image he could not escape. It was in every mirror he looked into, in every window he went past it hung like a mask. It was a pale, frightened face, cruelly marked with festering sores by an insidious disease. Under the throttling pressure of his wrists the face was filled with an impotent fear that was forcing her eyes out of their sockets. And out of her gasping throat her decomposing tongue came creeping like an entrail, endless, growing longer and longer, bigger and bigger until it broke through the glass of the windows he had to pass. The street was aimless and long, the poisonous tongue was stretching out towards him, licking at

9

his coat, coming closer and closer. Oh, dear God! There it was! Away, and for God's sake don't turn round!

Daniel Jesus was running, scurrying along with short, jerky steps, and the sweat ran down in pale drops into his sparse beard. He ran until his diseased lung forced him to come to a rasping halt. He leant against a lamp-post and rested. Thank God, the panic had passed, he no longer felt afraid. He really should go and see a doctor soon, he was having visions. The evening wasn't dead at all, it was still going down the street in front of him, dancing a polka round each of the electric lamps, skipping scornfully from one side of the street to the other, peeping into the ground-floor apartments. He hadn't strangled it, that was why there was no need to be frightened of that face. But he would strangle it if he could, and damn the consequences, even if the foul face should drive him to his grave. He hated evening. It had made fun of his hunchback in a hundred shadows on the walls of the houses, distorted and grotesque caricatures, comic and mean.

Every time he came to a lamp he could see his hunchback with its crooked point reflected two or three times on the wall and on the ground, in many different variations of shade and shape. The sun was honest and showed him his defect, but the evening mocked it. He would not be mocked! He was Daniel Jesus, a man of wealth and substance to whom, if he wanted, people bowed low and kissed his hand.

With bitter groans he continued on his way. The life he was leading was no life at all. It had no goal, no end, just like the road stretching out in front of him. It consisted of nothing but dreary dissipation, a hollow sham with nothing to satisfy the cravings of a deep-feeling heart. The orgy he had given in his house last night for young Baron Sterben's twentieth birthday, did it have the grandeur, the cruelty, even the slightest flicker of the great glory of iniquity? Fire and sin? Destruction? No and no! It had not even been shameless. A few naked girls who had got drunk on champagne and been sick on his beautiful, blood-red carpet that was worth a king's ransom. Where in that was the blind infamy that would alone be worthy of him? He should have found a princess! A princess of the soul, chaste and pure, to give the whole affair a touch of tragedy, a hint of force, violation and sin. There should have been a saint sitting on his knees, stark naked, strewing roses over his ugly hunchback with her white hands, kissing his deformed feet and offering Baron Sterben a glass of champagne. But all it had been was stupid and boring. These little bourgeoises had no soul. Nothing moved them, nothing roused them, they felt no thrill at such an evening. Nothing screamed out inside them, nothing froze, there was no crime, no great wickedness, no ecstasy of self-abasement, no intoxication and no yearning.

He needed to see souls when they were naked and drunk. He loved that. Fuddled and fervent, debauched and delirious. Driven out of their minds by a god or a beast. That was why he was heading for the little house by the railway viaduct where he had not been for a long time. He would get a chilly reception from them, from Anton the cobbler and his band of worshippers. They always knew everything he did. They were like his bad conscience. They would certainly already know that he had sinned again the previous evening, that he had opened his doors to the Devil. How Anton found out all these things was a mystery to him, but find them out he did.

In a fever of apprehension he climbed the wooden steps. He opened the door quietly and entered the room.

They were singing a hymn to Mary, the hymn of the sorrowing heart. Round a long, bare wooden table a crowd of people were standing with hymn-books in their hot hands; their voices rose up like a bitter, broken cry, wearing themselves hoarse against the low ceiling. All their hearts were filled with the hymn alone; they scarcely had room in their souls for anything happening outside. At the head of the table stood Anton, the cobbler. He knew the hymn by heart, had folded his immense, hard red hands in prayer and was singing. It was like a distress call at sea. His ship had been wrecked in the dark night of sin, was drifting rudderless, seeking God. He called out into the darkness, ceaselessly, louder and louder, senselessly, trustingly. The head on top of his massive body

11

was wild and proud; defiantly, austerely clean-shaven and with a mouth that was like a sword-cut in his scarred face.

Beside him stood his wife. As tall and massive as the cobbler, with wonderful, flaming, fiery red hair. She twisted and bent her powerful body as she sang, wrestling with sin. She shouted out the song into the room so that it tumbled out into the street like a lost, strangled sobbing that made the old women shiver and cross themselves. But it was to no avail. She could not silence the throbbing of her blood, the hymn did not fill her heart as it did the hearts of the others. Even between the verses she felt herself yearning for a devouring fire. Her love for God was puny and weak, it was not a raging storm, as was Anton's love. He was a messiah and redeemer and she was a poor, weak woman. But she needed a fire to burn in her soul and make her blood dry up, like a puddle in the sun. There was much within her that needed a purifying flame. She hated her blood and her great body, which she could not subdue. She felt a dull, lustful fear of her body. She sang, it was like a distress call at sea.

'Christ! Christ!' came the cry within her.

She sent her wide, devouring eyes along the smoky walls and past the contorted faces of the congregation, but the hymn would not fill her soul.

Then all at once, among the dreams and visions, the flames and phantasms of her singing, she suddenly saw, like the shadow behind a candle, Daniel Jesus standing in the room. He looked at her and her eyes were absorbed. Naked and shameless, like a woman entering her lover's bed, her eyes entered his. And sin, huge and ugly like the evening outside that Daniel Jesus could not catch, stepped into the hymn. Daniel Jesus felt as if an icy hand were passing over his hunchback. He drank in the look from the penitent like a beautiful, base iniquity. He knew that there was a princess heading towards him. She was still far off, and her horses were travelling slowly.

But the evening will bring us together, Anton. For the evening is evil.

No one had seen the shameless look apart from the

groaning gypsy woman lying on the floor before Anton, scraping her knees on the bare boards until the blood ran down. Her lips covered in foam, she kissed the cobbler's feet, straightened up and pounced on his hard hands; she was as hot as boiling snow.

But his hands did not pull back. He raised her up, high and alone above all the people, higher and higher, far beyond them, to God.

2

Baron Sterben was a very good man and a very bad man. He was completely unaware of it. The good within him was the source of all the noble impulses which even he at times loved about himself; the bad gave his soul a particular mean and shabby note which he was often at a loss to understand. He himself took no active part in all this. He did not resist the evil within him, nor did he do anything to encourage his finer side. He was twenty years old and had already seen through the glittering façade of life to its sterile depths. Now he went along with anything that had a taste of the singular, the aloof, with any adventure as long as the price was high, with any sin, if he still found a thrill in it. That is to say, it was not he who did all that, it was the things themselves whose lives were carried on through his, who passed through him as through an open door. Sometimes his soul did something, his hand or someone else, but never he himself; he believed he had lost his self in the unhealthy dreams of his youth. He was passive, and the days did with him as they liked.

He loved Hagar, the young gypsy girl. He had discovered her a few weeks ago at a fair outside the city where she performed childish jigs for the grubby coppers the people threw her. She had attracted him because she danced barefoot and was small and lean, like a wildcat. By the time had been watching her for fifteen minutes he was shivering, he knew that it was all in vain, that his poor body, tormented by love, would compel him to possess her. She had large, thin gold rings in her ears over which her hair fell like a curtain. For years now large, slim rings framing a pale woman's face had been his fetish. It was a wild, rainy day in early spring and his teeth were chattering feverishly. He was dimly, hopelessly aware that there was something dangerous and evil in Hagar's eyes, something that was destined to torment his young life like the lash of a scourge. But it was precisely that which, leaden, ineluctable, imperious, cast its spell over him. There was no escaping it.

Thus Hagar became the Baron's mistress.

She had gone with him in mute amazement. She did not quite know what to do with this man whose lips twitched as he spoke to her, whose features were shuddering under waves of fever like corn in the wind. He was delighted that she was called Hagar, it was a name that had captivated him at school, the fate of the Biblical Hagar had touched him as if she had been his own mother. Now she was to be his mistress and he was taking her to his house. He had bought her for a hundred crowns from a greasy showman who would have presumably been happy with twenty, so hungry he was, having gone without meat for days.

She walked through the streets beside him, quiet and submissive, and the people looked round and smiled when they recognised the Baron. She was wearing a faded dark-red dress and went barefoot. When they reached his home, he picked her up in his arms and sang a little, slightly ironic tune he had once heard from a woman at a strange moment in his life. With the tip of his patent-leather shoe he pushed open a beautiful, wide door and lay the mute Hagar down on his bed of silk. He pushed a costly, sad, deep-blue pillow under her brown neck, then knelt down by the bed and, breathing slowly, began to take off her clothes, one by one.

At that Hagar turned her head towards him and looked at him. Then she uttered some words that swept over the hot skin of his face like a caress. He gave a cry and kissed her with all the sickly fervour of his body, shattered under the impact of love. He kissed her until the blood ran down from her lips onto the white polar-bearskin on which he was kneeling. Then he took hold of her with both hands and tore apart the shift over her heaving breast so that she lay there naked before him, completely his.

Since then many weeks had passed, weeks during which she had tormented him with her love, had made him the slave of her small, thin body, which was slowly destroying him. Hagar was ruthless and without pity. She would dig her

15

brown, trembling fingers into his soft flesh and bite at his chest like a cat until she drew blood. Her demanding, uninhibited love was like a deep dream in which he was enmeshed beyond hope of waking.

Then one day Daniel Jesus came and drove her out of Baron Sterben's house with a whip. He did not want his young friend destroyed by this debauched witch. The Baron's heart had something great, something fantastic about it that Daniel Jesus wanted to preserve and that the gypsy girl stole every night he spent desperately wrestling with her body, as with an animal.

At first he let out a cry and tried to tear the whip out of Daniel Jesus' hand, then he threw himself to the ground, pulled the rug over his head and let him have his way.

Hagar came back, but she no longer tortured him. By day she sat, darkly mute, in a corner, and by night she talked with her dreams. Once she asked him to read to her from an old, stained book. He was amazed to find it full of prayers, hymns, sacred texts and an ancient litany to a long-forgotten saint. There was a blind, unyielding fervour in the hymns, a wild yearning, the sense of an ultimate stage, marked by the cross.

He asked her.

She answered defiantly that now she was going to Anton, the cobbler, the holy man who lived out beyond the station, in the long street with the hundred lamps. She was a sinner, she said, and had to pray, for hours on end, every day, so that God would forgive her and she would find peace.

'Peace?' He was taken aback by the word.

'Peace? Does the cobbler promise peace?'

'Yes.'

Then she spent a whole hour telling him about the messiah. How great and powerful he was, like a king among all people; how at the sound of his voice every sin fell silent; how his hands rose up high towards God; how he proclaimed the coming of the millenium. People should flee one another, he said, for in company was sin. Where two were gathered together, there let God stand between them so that their naked eyes might not see, that they need not be ashamed; that we might no longer be poor and troubled, struggling with ourselves and the world; that we might not succumb to the desperate torments of lust; that we might be free of all longing, except of our longing for God; that we might have no desire but for God. Cursed be all love that would bypass God. He takes all consciousness from such love, so that it can do nothing but babble its own torment.

She had talked herself into a heat. Her cheeks were burning, her hair had come loose and was falling over her face. At that moment she was beautiful, the gypsy girl, and he put his arm round her to kiss her. Since the day when Daniel Jesus had taken the whip to her he had not touched her. Lust reawoke within him, and he was trembling, just as on that wild, rainy spring day when he had first seen her dancing barefoot before him.

'Hagar', he stammered hoarsely, and tried to kiss her.

But she turned aside from him and pushed him away. And when he seized her round the waist, she screamed, as if in terror. At that a blazing, bright-red wave of blood roared through his skull like a steam train. He grabbed the gypsy girl by the feet and threw her to the ground, placed his knee on her squirming body and tried to tear the dress off her breast, as he had done when she first came to the house. Then she raised her hand and hit him hard, in a blind fury, across the face, three or four times. He let go and looked down at her, pale with horror, as at an animal.

Then he gave a laugh and sneered, 'You're in love with your cobbler; you don't like me any more. Why don't you go to him, he's big and strong; his bed is wide, you can pray there.'

She was still lying on the floor. 'That's not true!' she cried. Then there was a pause, during which they looked at each other, and each could hear the whispering of the other's blood; a moment during which their eyes widened in anguish and filled with tears glistening with the sadness of their wounded souls.

'That's not true!' She howled like a dog, then flung her head to the ground and burst into tears. The joy, in which she had believed for many days, had been taken from her; it had shrivelled up inside her, and nothing could revive it. All at once she realised that she had never sought God in the cobbler's shack; she loved Anton and lusted after him, only she had not been aware of it. Now it had suddenly become clear to her that she yearned for his huge, proud body, for his ugly mouth with the flaming scars. And he was God's and would crush her if she went to him.

That was why the gypsy girl was crying.

3

The voices of the restless March day, full of foreboding, had penetrated the heavy silk curtains over the doors of Countess Regina's drawing room, making her pensive and unsure of herself. These voices pervaded her soul like some apprehensive, dangerous treachery, and at times she felt that they were talking about her. That was something she did not want; she wanted to be old and to live out the rest of her days without a struggle, in her love for Martha Bianca.

It was very quiet today, no one spoke a word. All five were looking each other in the eye, waiting for something. Regina was sitting in a deep, immensely soft rocking chair, occasionally throwing little sidelong smiling glances at a mirror sleeping in a corner, hidden in the dark folds of the curtains. She looked at the strands of white at her temples and gave a soft laugh. Martha Bianca was sitting at her feet, pale and dutiful, her amber hair welling up towards her mother in a cascade of light. Baron Sterben looked at it, amazed at the way Martha Bianca's presence almost lit up the drawing room. Whenever she fixed her large, velvety child's eyes on him, he was reminded of a lamp burning with a beautiful, dreamy flame, soft and gentle, yet full of a sweet, veiled fire.

Her body must be silvery white, he dreamed, and gave a start as Martha Bianca slowly stood up and left the drawing room.

Then suddenly Countess Regina, her eyes fixed so firmly on the young actor, Valentin, that he went pale, said, as if she had just remembered something, 'Why don't you tell us the story of little Valeska, my dear Daniel Jesus? How she almost strangled you once while you were asleep?'

Daniel Jesus looked up. The whole time he had been sitting on the gleaming carpet that covered the floor, encircling the broad feet of the table with fantastic lines of colour that reached out towards the walls. Daniel Jesus always sat on the floor, and Regina tolerated his habit with a pitying smile, as long as there was no stranger present who might question it with a wondering glance. He did not feel at ease on the high chairs and pieces of furniture on which other people sat and on which he had to dangle his thin legs like a child. At such times he felt everyone was looking at his back and had to put up with it, without being able to scratch their inquisitive eyes out. That was why he preferred to squat on the floor somewhere where all glances passed above him, somewhere he could remain in the darkness like a breathing shadow, only his gigantic head occasionally breaking the surface when he spoke.

He must have been sitting there in silence for a good fifteen minutes, observing with a mocking half-smile on his lips the Baron's private game with the twelve-year-old Martha Bianca and the pointless hostilities between Regina and Valentin. The young actor had a head like a Hun, broad, bony, with sunken cheeks and almost grotesquely deep-lying, scorching eyes. The tall, slim countess with her poised, effortless gestures and her severe white hands which still seemed to contain a flicker of repressed sensuality, was an enigma to him, an enigma he was burning to solve. Regina was a little afraid of him, and this fear was like the lascivious prick of a goad that kept driving her back to him. Today, from the street outside, the half-spoken words and voices of the March day had penetrated her drawing room like a mysterious, distant cry shredded by the wind. She was restless and defiant; she slowly raised her tired pupils from his twitching feet to his face and stared at him with the steady beam of a lamp.

'Tell me about Valeska, Daniel, please', said the countess. 'He must tell us the story, mustn't he, Baron?'

Sterben had been dreaming of a young forest, the leaves waving like blond hair, the trees tall and slim. Spring was galloping through the woods like a white stallion, without saddle or reins, maddened, foaming at the nostrils. Up above, the sky was hanging down over the young trees, yellow and full of sun like a girl's amber tresses. He went on until he came to a beech tree with its bark hanging down in pieces. Red, quivering blood was running out of the trunk to which a child was bound with straps and chains, a naked, silver-white, tortured body. He shrank back in horror and ran on, out of the forest, into a clearing, into a field, and he looked up at Countess Regina and said, 'Yes, Countess, yes.'

So Daniel Jesus wrapped his long arms round his knees and began:

'Valeska was very young when I seduced her, scarcely a year older than Martha Bianca, I think. She was the daughter of one of the clerks from my factory. At first she visited me secretly, and when her father discovered it he beat her for an hour with such a heavy stick that he broke her left arm. After that she lived permanently with me. They threatened to take me to court for seducing a girl below the age of consent, but ultimately they didn't dare and so Valeska stayed in my house. I can't say that she loved me, but she feared me, and it was not Valeska herself, it was her fear that was the slave that brought me her love. In me she feared the man who had been the first to light the fire in her soul and in her blood which, at the age of thirteen, she only half understood, but which had already destroyed her happiness, a considerable portion of her life, the blissful smile of sleep and the hushed peace of her heart. She did not love me, but she gave herself to me with a frenzied abandon and tears, in which there was not a drop of regret, nor the least ounce of strength to envisage anything beyond the immediate present. She had forgotten she was in a world where there were perhaps a thousand days, a thousand weeks before her, awaiting the sound of her voice. She had nothing to say to life, and in the loneliness and helplessness of her heart she fell ill. Her soul withered in the darkness. She searched for love, but in vain. What could she find to love in me? I was a hunchback. I was brutal. There was no one else she knew. Her heart froze and her soul disintegrated. She started stealing money and silver from the house, even though I gave her everything she wanted. When I learnt of it I beat her as mercilessly as her father had. I was brutal and left her lying on the floor unconscious. After that she became worse, even more recalcitrant, and would not speak a word to me for days on end.

21

Once I woke up. It was a bright, singing night. The moon had tumbled through the open summer window into my room; it was as if I had it all to myself there in the room and outside it had completely disappeared, so dazzlingly bright and clear was everything around me. The drawer from my desk in the adjoining room lay on the floor, completely empty, and beside my bed – I could just see it out of the corner of my eye – was a large bundle of banknotes that I had concealed in it. Before me was Valeska, standing there in her nightdress which had slipped down over her shoulders so that I could see her nipples. In the white light they stood out blood red, like two wounds. She had her left hand round my throat, and the warm blood that her nails were gouging out of my veins was already trickling down my skin. In her right hand she was holding my dagger, razor-edged and beautifully fashioned, with a large, dark ruby on the hilt, like a bloody tear-drop clinging to it. She was about to kill me, and if I had woken up a second later she would have cut my heart in two. I gave a scream and kicked her in the belly, knocking her to the floor.

I stood up and dressed. She was still lying on the floor beside my bed, her skin damp with sweat.

"Why were you going to do that?" I asked at last.

She raised her head and looked at me out of lifeless night eyes. "I hated you and wanted to kill you. I stole your money and was going to run away. Do what you like." '

Daniel Jesus was silent. He looked at the long lines of the carpet as if staring into a dream and his fingers closed in a gesture as if he were putting the bygone hours behind him for ever.

'And what did you do?' asked the Countess

'It was the most precious night of my whole life. In Valeska's eyes I saw everything anyone ever said to me, or ever will. In her eyes I recognised myself, woman, fate and love. And in those eyes I found the path that leads between thorns and sorrow to happiness and peace. I took her in my arms and kissed her. I kissed her brow, her hands, her mouth.

And it was as if a miracle were happening to Valeska. All her harshness, coarseness, dullness dissipated like a mist and turned into radiance, goodness and painful devotion in that summer night. I picked up the money from the floor and gave it to her.

"I'm going to build you a house with high windows and exquisite rooms, Valeska. It is to be yours and you shall live in it."

Slowly the tears came, painfully slowly. They came like spring to her parched soul, her heart bloomed red like a rose.

"No, no", she said, and went out. In that moment she loved me and it was still no help to us. I never saw her again. She beat out her own brains on her father's door.'

For a whole, long half hour the ticking of the clock paced round the room like a someone in a dream going down a sleeping street. No one said a word. Daniel Jesus looked out of the window where, in a low voice, the March wind was singing the songs of yearning the servant girls sing. Martha Bianca came back in quietly and sat down silently at the piano. Then she played some piece or other, a long melody, full of danger, in which her flying amber tresses were mingled like flames.

None of the men in the room was musical, but they were all drawn under a spell in which the Countess' fear, Valentin's longing, the Baron's dreams and the story of Valeska and her death merged with the wild, menacing notes of the music into a dark, ambiguous picture.

4

Anton had a son. When he was still a child, the cobbler had called him Joseph, but for years now he had not spoken a single word to him. He had paid for him to attend college, hoping he would grow up to be sensible and hard-working. Instead he had gone bad. Only a few weeks ago he had come out of prison again. He slipped quietly into his room, so that no one could hear him, and avoided everyone. His father and Margaret, his mother, suffered him to stay in their house because he was their son; in the evenings they prayed for his soul while he spent all his money on drink in low taverns.

During the day Joseph worked as a clerk for a small-time lawyer. Pale and taciturn, he did what that was asked of him and sullenly pocketed his meagre wage each month. It was Daniel Jesus who had found him the position because he was interested in the young man with the grubby slouch hat, a green stone in the pin in his gaudy tie and the face of a thief. Daniel Jesus' steely, far-seeing eye saw through to people's souls. He did not categorise them according to their usefulness and their value in the world, rather he generally saw and was on his guard against the latent forces of destiny whose instruments they were. From the very first he had recognised in Joseph that grandiose, unconscious, blind, raging energy that had dragged his youth down into darkness and filth. He knew that Joseph was one of those rare individuals who could be used to accelerate destinies, to make tentative developments explode brutally into foolhardy and painful blossomings. Joseph would be capable of setting fire to a town and killing a thousand people in the blaze, if someone suggested the idea to him while he was drunk. He was weak but violent, unsure of himself and lacking in self-confidence, but obstinate and cruel in his heart.

The discovery of this man had filled Daniel Jesus with horror and delight. He supported him with money and used his influence to keep the police away from him as far as possible.

He was keeping him, as he occasionally admitted to himself with a prickle of fear, for one of the great, red moments of his life in which the drunken hand of the thief would bring to him, amid fire, dust and ashes, a word, an experience which would never have come, or not for a long time, without him. He was beginning to feel that that moment was within reach. He looked at the cobbler's son and saw his pale, scarred brow over which there crept the base thoughts of a cowardly, reckless heart, saw the shadows and blotches on his face which spoke of the wild curses of his dazed soul. He knew that this creature was ripe for him. The realisation came over him almost like a chill of fear.

Daniel Jesus was rich. He scattered his money around him with the feverish hands of someone who is emperor for just a few minutes. Because of that he seemed to exert a magic power over others. He was often reminded of the Pied Piper of Hamelin. His money drew an invisible, ghostly circle around him which no one who came within its orbit could escape. Many people had already been betrayed because of him, many a person's happiness sold. And yet wherever he was, he was still surrounded by intoxication and supine abandon. When musicians played for him, it was as if their instruments came alive, grew hands of their own. They spoke and shouted at him in a thousand scraps of melody, pursued him, snatched at him with their fingers, begged, laughed and suddenly fell silent. Then they danced around him, always giggling when they passed behind him and saw his hunchback, with ringing, insolent laughter, like the boys who laughed at him in the street.

Daniel Jesus sat on the filthy floorboards and screamed. He wanted a different song, an honest or a rascally song, but not one that crept up behind him with a twisted grin on its face and made such a fiendishly shrill jingling with his own money. Black Carmen was sitting before him on an empty barrel. She had rings as thick as her fingers in her ears with a genuine diamond in each. Daniel Jesus had given her the diamonds last summer because she had amused him for a quarter of an hour. She had driven through the town in the middle of the day in his own carriage, sitting up on the coach-box, stark naked. With his two wildest horses harnessed, she had raced through the streets like a Maenad, and no one had dared to stop her in her frenzied gallop. By chance there were no accidents and the police were powerless to do anything about it. People had recognised Daniel Jesus' carriage, but no one could make a definite statement. So Black Carmen, the naked whore, had driven with exultant whoops in through the wide-open gates of 'Jesus Villa', and the old beggar-woman in the street and the hurdy-gurdy man with his wooden leg had stared after the carriage and its driver as if they had seen a ghost.

Today Daniel Jesus had no thought for that exploit. He was staring at the red, haggard face of Joseph, the clerk, as he danced with the silk-clad Rosa among pimps and whores. He was in a sordid wine-and-schnapps cellar that was below the ground in the very same building where Anton lived. One only had to go out of the low-ceilinged room, where the fumes from the oil-lamps were like a yellow wall between the noisy drinkers and dancers, to see the damp stairs that led steeply up through the dark to the cobbler's door. Anton was not at home. He had gone with a throng of his devotees to a village where a girl saw the Mother of God every day. That was someone he had to see. That very night the men had set out to find her.

Margaret was alone in her bed in the darkness, wrestling with her flesh. She was clutching the iron crucifix in her hands, and it was almost red-hot from her feverish grip. Just as during the meeting in their room, when she had stood beside her husband singing the hymn to Mary, she was crying out to God in the torment of her struggle, and her breast was hot and wet from the sweat of fear. She was afraid of sin, of the sin that had accompanied her through the years, blowing the caustic ash of discontent into all her prayers and all her acts. So far she had always emerged victorious, and Anton, her husband, took her by the arm when she stumbled and could not see the way ahead clearly. And was she to succumb now, now that she had grown old and had a son of twenty-four?! Her son! She shuddered. O God, why had he punished her in that way?! Yes, yes, that was the sin that was within her and refused to die, the sin that cried out in her blood and made her massive body rear up, as if in convulsions.

Margaret listened for the sounds from below. From deep, deep down in the cellar there sometimes came to her a noise like the growling breath of some animal; or the cry of a violin, finding no escape from the walls of the building, would flee as one pursued up the dark stairs to collapse to the floor beside Margaret's bed like a weary soul. That was where he spent every evening! He would not even make the effort to take his shame away from his mother's house. She could hear the panting of his soul, for which she prayed tortured prayers, rising up from the smoke and filth even to her room.

Suddenly she closed her eyes. In the blackness of the night her face turned as white as a dream. *He* was down there, he too! She had seen his carriage standing outside the house, she could hear the horses pawing the ground with their hooves. Daniel Jesus! 'Mother of God', she cried, 'save me, save me from sin. He is a cripple and ugly as sin, but I fear the love I have for him, and there is no one here to hold my hand in my hour of need.'

Drunkenness had taken hold of the people in the cellar below. It laughed and tripped over its own feet and stared at the window-panes with its weak, glazed, red eyes as if it was looking for an object on which to vent its hidden, repressed anger.

Daniel Jesus was staring straight at the drunken Joseph, who had unbuttoned Rosa's bodice and was biting at her red, sweaty breasts, while she squawked and pushed him away from her. Daniel Jesus could see the garish green stone glittering at his throat, could see the faint flicker of his eyelids in which his weakness was revealed, could see his intemperate, sensuous lips.

'The ultimate hour', he thought, and called the clerk over.

'You have a beautiful mother, Joseph,' he said.

'Yes, and if you want her, I'll bring her to you', Joseph babbled drunkenly.

The shadow of a powerful, compelling emotion passed over Daniel Jesus' features. A hundred old, pale thoughts let out a sigh and shrivelled up. In the deepest recesses of his soul he had always been afraid of Joseph, thinking perhaps in supporting him he was preparing the instrument of his own doom, just as one might mix a fatal drink for one's own death. But now he felt a sense of release. Now he knew that nothing could impede his fulfilment. His mouth twisted in an arrogant smile.

'Go! Fetch her!' he said. 'She's sleeping alone in her bed. I want to see her body, naked, with no clothes on. Tell her that. And if she will not comply, use force. I will give you a fortune. But be careful, she is a powerful woman.'

At that the drunk man's eyes grew wide, deep, unfocused, like the eyes of a blind man. A shiver ran through his body, a cry, then he flew off up the stairs.

And suddenly, as if someone had signalled to them, the band stopped playing. The players crouched together in a huddle. Black Carmen opened her mouth wide and fell unconscious to the floor, legs flung apart. In the middle of the room stood Daniel Jesus, as steadfast, as assured as a king, despite his hunchback.

For a quarter of an hour and more he stood there. 'A struggle', he thought. Then suddenly, in the silence that had made even the oil lamps go pale and timid, came the sound of someone coming down the stairs. Slow, heavy steps, dogged and futile. Like a clumsy, sticky lump that can hardly move from the spot. Then the door flew open wide with a screech of terror and in came Joseph, his hair plastered in blood and sweat, a jagged cut running right across his cheek from which the blood poured down like water from a broken jug.

He dragged in his naked mother by the hair and threw her at Daniel Jesus' feet.

She leapt up and stood there, her face blazing, beautiful, her hair wreathed round her head like a crown. She drew up her powerful, naked body, letting the drunken crew around her see her magnificent, shining skin and the scars where birth had torn her flesh. Her eyes were almost invisible in the

28

fierceness of the light they gave off as she asked, 'Who did this?'

There was a wide, whispering pause, during which Black Carmen gave a groan and raised her right hand.

'I did', said Daniel Jesus.

A shudder went through Margaret's body, a savage, feverish shivering.

Daniel Jesus knelt down, kissed her feet and said, 'I love you. I am master of your life, for I know that you love me too. You cannot fight me, I am stronger than you. Seven days I will wait. Then come to my villa outside the town when evening has fallen. Be sure to come. I desire it.'

5

Martha Bianca had heard poor Valeska's story after all. No one knew that she had been standing by the half-open door of the adjoining room and that the words from Daniel Jesus' lips had fallen like large, blossoming drops into the open sore of her longing.

Since that hour his tale never left her. It lay over her soul, enmeshing it in a closely woven, shimmering net, and would not let go of her. She sometimes felt that those events were oppressing her in some important yet undefined way, were taking her through long labyrinths of love of which no one had ever spoken to her but which she still saw in a bright, clear light, like the story of a vision.

Martha Bianca was a fanciful child. Her mother had enveloped her young life in a cloak of meek quietness, but underneath it, slowly, strangely, red smoke had wreathed up round her soul in which she saw fantastic figures and objects. When she was sitting in the darkening drawing room in the late afternoon and the countess was reading a book, she would look over to the huge window-panes, which the weary sun set on fire with a clear, bright flame and beyond which was the cold street and its adventures. Gradually some other life, new to her, would unfold before her inner eye, with a hundred incidents and desires which meshed and complemented each other as in a novel. People she had met some time or other would appear, but when she looked more closely at them, they had different faces. They had grown old, or they had something about them that took her by surprise and made her stare in astonishment: an imperious, unrestrained manner, sudden gestures expressing remorse or hatred, love or guile. At times it happened that Martha Bianca would forget her own life, her mother and the lonely room where she lived, and would go out into the world with one of the people she saw in her mind's eye, someone with grave, menacing hands who was speaking into the red air, as if there was someone behind him. Or she would become one of those people herself, experiencing some destiny which another had created out of cunning or cruelty and in which she acted out her part as if in a game.

Daniel Jesus' tale had pierced this heart like a gleaming knife, killing all her own experiences and their reflections in a confused dream in which she was suddenly running away from Martha Bianca in mute despair along a path which led, beyond rocks and bloody shadows, to Valeska's death.

The dull, dreary hours of abstinence and fear were transmuted within her into a power of longing and release which made her ripen into love, like a tree in which the breath of God is sleeping. This love confused her memory and carried her beyond the end and the sadness of Daniel's story. She knew, with a pang of sorrow, that Valeska had died, but her eyes probed the velvet curtain of night in unbelief, and her soul felt impelled to speak. She saw that great, that precious moment when Daniel Jesus, with tears of happiness, had kissed her weeping lips, that moment in which everything became manifest and her life had been touched by wonder for the first time in years.

Perhaps his life too – that was Valeska thinking. He had played with brightly coloured cinders, with the glittering baubles of his heart. It had not brought him happiness. But that was what he must have! She had to take him the love that was his, that very night. She was not dead, who had made up that lie? She had just had a bad dream, and now it was over.

It was a soaring, radiant night, just like the one Daniel Jesus had described. The moon had unrolled a marvellous, yearning carpet over her bedroom floor and only her bed was left in darkness. She got up and jumped down into the room in her nightdress. Her feet were in the light, and her face, pale, passive, expectant, was half veiled by her amber hair. Then, hesitantly and with tiny, childlike steps, she went over to the old rococo chest and took out a soft, shimmering cloak of a tranquil, dreamy silk, while her feet fled from the light of the moon into two tiny, dark blue slippers. She wrapped the cloak round her nightdress and pushed the door open. Soundlessly she slipped through the house, felt her way down the stairs and unlocked the front door with a heavy iron key.

The breeze was winging its way through the street. It was voluptuously warm. Spring had poured a glistening shower over the churches and roofs of the town, and now and then came the sound of late March calling out some clear but far-off cry. High above, the moon was floating along on the back of the quivering wind, like a bride waiting for her wedding day.

Martha Bianca was running. She did not know where she was running to. All she had, at the back of her mind, was the vague image of a bright, slender house she had once driven past in the carriage with her mother, who had said something about it that she had since forgotten. And then? But she wasn't the girl in the carriage at all. Who could it have been? – Wasn't it Martha Bianca? – Martha Bianca – of course! She had loved her very much once upon a time; she was a quiet girl, a dreamer, but still very young, much too young for love.

Where was she going? She was Valeska and she had to take her love to someone, that very night. He didn't know yet what she was bringing him.

She smiled.

He will be amazed, she thought, not noticing that the street had stolen her delicate slippers wrought with sad pearls and that she was running over the cobbles in her bare feet.

He would be happy. He would kiss her. Never again would she go and beat out her brains as she had done in that night. She would stay with him and never leave him. He was kind, he had the eyes of a child; he would find the way to peace.

He –? But who was it? A gust of wind came, sending icy shivers through her. Good God, she had completely forgotten that! Love had confused her, love had made her mad. She could feel the sobs rising in her throat. Hastily, anxiously she searched through her dreams, crying. There she was, standing barefoot in the street, with nothing on but her nightdress and cloak, and did not know to whom she was going.

But was she not Valeska? In that case she must go to Daniel Jesus. Yes, that was it, now she remembered. He had told her mother the story. She stood in a doorway, listening. Her feet were tired and weary, as if she were ill.

To Daniel Jesus, then, she thought. But what was that? That wasn't right. He wasn't the one she loved. The one she loved was different. He was young and handsome and had yearning lips. Sometimes a flush of fever would pass over his face and his eyes became fixed, as in a dream.

Martha Bianca looked up. Before her was a house, bright and slender, with silver windows. She turned the knob, the door opened. She was surprised that it was not locked, but then she remembered that it could not be otherwise since her life was an enchanted dream. The night and her love were as they were because they had to be.

Softly she climbed the stairs and went into the room.

But who is it I'm going to? she asked herself in bitter despondency, closing the door behind her.

Then she was standing, beautiful and silent, in the white room looking into Baron von Sterben's wide eyes which, until a moment ago, had been filled with dreams. She was standing on the polar-bear skin by his bed, her bare foot crushing the blood that had trickled from Hagar's lips as the Baron kissed her. Her soft, delicate cloak opened, and Baron Sterben could see that she had come to him barefoot, wearing only her nightdress. Her yellow hair fell over her eyes as she said, 'The street door was open so I came up. But how is it that you do not lock the door when you're sleeping?'

A peal of bright laughter went through the Baron's soul. 'Martha Bianca!' he cried. 'Martha Bianca – I have left it unlocked for years – for happiness to come in.'

6

In the night in which Daniel Jesus played his great, reckless game with Margaret's love, Anton brought a strange, marvellous, confused girl back from the village. Blond and as thin as a saint, she talked to no one, nor did she do anything. The people in the village, who did not believe in her dreams, were glad when the cobbler took her, since she was an orphan and they did not know what to do with her. Now she was living in his house. Anton's tiny community loved her. They listened in humble reverence to the experiences of her inner life when, during the long prayer meetings, among the hymns and the mad, ecstatic cries of the cobbler's wife, she would fall, serenely smiling, into a beautiful, hot sleep and then talk with harsh, chapped lips of the image that shone down into her life day after day, like the light from a radiant mirror. Often, when the cobbler came to her and held her fluttering hands, it was as if a cloud were passing over her dream. Then, in a hoarse, halting voice, she would speak of a mighty, evil messiah of sin who had established his kingdom alongside Anton's, and who would destroy the Kingdom of God. She prophesied the advent of gaudy, disjointed days, which were almost upon them, when they would all pant under the lashes of Satan's whip, as if a storm had blown away all their prayers.

'Then the evil foe will pronounce his heart's dominion over you like a curse. None will be missing from his retinue. None.

Not even you!

Not even you!'

She shouted her final words at the cobbler's deathly pale face, then collapsed unconscious into his arms.

On such evenings a shudder of horror went through the souls of the assembled congregation. They were afraid beyond words of the things the girl spoke of in her ecstatic trance, afraid of the day that would once more block their path to peace, of the day when once more they would be poor and tormented, stumbling along in the darkness, giddy with fear and despair. Where is this enemy? the scream went up inside them. Let us find him – and kill him!

Slowly, like a gurgling stream of black blood flowing over their eyes and hands, a name struggled to escape from their lips like a soft moaning:

'Christ! Christ!'

Margaret knew who the enemy was. And she could see his kingdom, just as the unconscious girl saw it, falling into their hearts, great, magnificent, dark, so that they were incapable of fighting against it. It came and came and they were all weary and disheartened, drained of all their strength. But within him was a force, steely and untamed, which spouted up from his soul in a triumphant jet, infamous and without shame, exulting in its own misdeeds, full of fire and sin and beauty. She did not know whether there had been a moment in his life when his soul had fled the crazed, flickering dance of his desires and sought refuge in a quiet which would take his racing heart in its calm, kind hands and show him the path they were all seeking, the path that led through love perhaps, or through God to peace. But that would have to be a painful, sacred love, appearing abruptly, born of wounds and dross. Margaret did not believe there had been such a moment in his life. She did not know the story of Valeska, she did not know the depths of his heart, deep as a moorland mire, where, among green, rocky dungeons, among the black, spectral shades of the stones and the eerie trails of the sea-sprite, there was a tiny house where for many long and wasted years a pale and strangely haggard face had pressed against the window-panes watching with the fading sight of yearning for the sea-sprite's ship. Even Daniel Jesus had almost forgotten that house and that window. His other yearning, great and foolish, was leading him somewhere, anywhere, on a rudderless route through the marvels and mock lights of delusion. Not to know where he was heading, where the reef was that would sink the sea-sprite's ship, held a strange, powerful attraction for his soul. In that bright, precious, moonlit night, Valeska's night, it had vanished from his anxious sight like the bark of the Flying Dutchman. It might never have returned; he might have lived long, long years in the house with the white window and his venturing yearning would have gone from him like a dream. But Valeska's blood would not have it so. Thus he journeyed further into the darkness, lighting his way with the red fires of his lusts and his deeds. His heart was strong, strong enough to overcome many. He could scatter the cobbler's kingdom as the storm blows away a flimsy vessel. What was *her* cry for help to him? He would take the cobbler's ageing wife a short way on his journey with him. He would take her fiery red hair like a torch through the evening which was full of dull, gaping fishes and strange clouds.

Margaret looked around her. She saw people lying breathing on the floor, cowardly and crushed. Her prayers rose to her lips like sobs and ran over her body, almost like a sensual touch. She stood there, looking down at the others. In four times twelve hours it would be seven days since Daniel Jesus had commanded her to come. She must deck herself out, she must be beautiful. She must comb her glowing, flame-red hair and wind it like a crown about her head once more. She would chastise her unbridled flesh for him so that his lusts would not find her blood empty and without fire, so that she could envelop his body in redness like a burning cloth.

The cobbler too was standing, straight and upright as a tree. He knew nothing of Margaret's struggle, he only sensed everything she was suffering when he heard her voice waver in the holy songs they sang in the evenings. Then a sadness and a compassionate severity came over him. Of her experiences that evening when she had stood before Daniel Jesus, naked and full of humility, quivering with love and shame, no one had said a word to him, and he did not ask. He had seen deep terror in his wife's eyes and waited for her to come and tell him everything. She had not come. She remained silent and he left her to her doubts. He felt a slight spurt of contempt for these people who who were at loggerheads with God and the devil, who could neither pray nor sin, and stood without light in the darkness, feeling their way with groping hands. Margaret was one of them, only she was better than the rest and did not lie on the floor like them. She stood up straight and was not afraid to let herself be shaken. How great he used to feel beside all these! He was strong, there was no fever in his soul. He raised his hands up, high above all the others and called out to God. So far God had always come and helped him bear his faith. He had believed that he really was the messiah of the poor and sick who cried at his feet like children. Not Christ, not a prophet, but a calm, strong man who could have led them through life to the end.

And now this girl came, this blond saint, her reason ruined by visions, and told him everything was in vain. Another, worse prophet had come to chastise them, and they would all bend their backs beneath his whip, in thrall and ready to serve him.

He too! He too!

Anton looked round. Everywhere he saw lips moving in prayer, hands trying to clasp each other in an appeal for grace. Where was this enemy? he wondered along with the rest. Where was he? A spasm of torment passed across his deathly pale face.

At his feet lay Hagar, the gypsy woman. Since the evening when she had hit the Baron across the face with her hand the poison in her blood had started a pernicious ferment. It seethed and foamed under her skin, stifling the laughter in her throat, it welled up from underneath her hot fingernails when, in lust and horror, she sank her teeth into her fingers. She had left the Baron's house that same evening, and since then no one knew where she ate or slept, or what she did. Every evening she came to the cobbler's when all the others were already there praying, and lay down on the floor beside him. She watched him as he spoke and sang, her eyes drinking in his every gesture, her lips, like a madwoman's, repeating every word he said to his God. She thirsted after his love.

Anton saw the gypsy woman. He saw her throw back her head and heard the gurgling coming from her taut, throbbing neck. Her saw her thin body arching itself up towards him like a cat's. And then it seemed as if he were looking into her eyes for the first time. Deep and glistening, they burnt into his cheek, his brow, his wide, ugly mouth. They sent fire and ice coursing through his body, making his prayers feeble, like those of a woman.

He was seized with a horror so futile, so monstrous that he cried out. The gurgling gypsy woman was writhing on the floor, kissing his feet. Her lips were covered in foam which spurted up, spattering the cobbler's hard hands, as hot as boiling snow.

With one kick he sent her far across the floor, sprawling among his praying followers.

That is the enemy! The thought flashed through his soul that was full of fear and trembling. He was lost, he felt it, but he drew up his body once more, tall and powerful, raised his huge red fists and cried, 'Never come again, gypsy woman, never again!'

Cowering, Hagar crept out through the door. And they knew that she would come again nevertheless. They all knew for they had all looked into her eyes and were afraid.

7

The sweat was like a cloud floating through the oppressive, quivering air. Their faces were flushed, and in their eyes lurked a dark resolve. The shadows of the dancers flickered and jagged across the green walls, one after the other, suddenly to be swallowed up in the blackness of the door. But they kept on coming back into the light, again and again, always the same, elongated, rushing, with hasty, forbidden gestures, urgent and impatient, with grotesque heads in a manic, contorted rhythm.

The wild keyboard was playing a waltz. Breathless and persistent, fast and tuneless. The notes climbed up into the stuffy air, up, up and up to the murky, indistinct ceiling, to fall down again in a steep, vertical plummet onto the floor amid the dancing couples, who crushed them beneath their hard, pitiless feet so that they cried out in fear and rage. There were a few strings missing in the body of the wild keyboard. It stood in the corner on its three legs, morose and querulous, and during the intervals, while the breath of the resting dancers beat a heavy, regular rhythm on the air, like the flail on the threshing-floor, it bared its grimy, vicious teeth at the world. The teeth of the piano were yellow and decayed, but sleeping within them was a discordant abyss of lust, an evil, inescapable torment of pleasure. When the squint-eyed musician touched its keys, its hoarse, repulsive voice called out enticingly; it cast a spell that grew and grew, ensnaring them all, shaking their longing from its slumber, shrilly calling it to life, with its most secret, most dangerous desires.

It was the people who came who called it the wild keyboard. They were a strange, motley crowd: young, pale, wanton youths with shifty, unbridled hands, and lewd, common women with greedy red lips and firm, thrusting breasts who stared at the walls as if in a deep dream and let the men almost carry them as they danced.

Again and again the wild keyboard played its only waltz, a

squealing tune with a heavy, thumping rhythm to which the crowd started to move slowly round the room. They were people of the night. A hundred reckless ideas surfaced, countless schemes and plans. Not mature and clearly articulated, such as come by day, but a tangle of aimless, obscure ideas that no one could unravel. Standing among the broad, bright columns the dust built up around the smoky lamps, the young men stared dully, drunkenly at their lives. The women closed their eyes, threw back their heads and saw nothing. They felt their bodies washed away by a thunderous, screaming wave, engulfing them in a hot, red sea. Under the influence of the drink, promises were given and faith was broken. Their minds were blank, they followed and were borne along, trembling with a yearning which erased every memory from their soul. Baneful words which had been lulled to sleep rose up and crushed them. And all the time the wild keyboard played its frenzied, fervent dances.

On the walls the blind, grotesque images of the people fluttered and disintegrated, only to leap up again and grasp each other in the whirling crowd. In the middle of it two shadows were flying through the light, unbridled and immersed in the fever like all the rest, but tall and beautiful among them. The woman was slender and supple, with fine, effortless hands which had great sensuality pent up in them; the man was young, strong and sombre with twitching, bony feet and a head like a buffalo. Their image flitted round the green walls, austere and ghostly, and all the black figures fled it, breathlessly hurrying away as if in some dark, mortal fear, and huddled by the door. The wild keyboard cried out in piercing laughter. Whenever the two shadows passed the piano, one threw a silver coin onto the squint-eyed musician's plate so that he plunged his fingers into the keys with an exultant cry and played on and on, without mercy, even though his song was over and the people were panting in the stifling air.

It was Valentin and Countess Regina dancing. She had suddenly gone off in the night with the young actor to this dance-floor where sin in its crudest form stammered out its revolting, drunken obscenities; where desires, freed from their chains, lurched round in circles, staring each other lasciviously in the face.

'Let's go there!' she had said when he told her about the place. He was still staring at her with a smile of disbelief as she stood up and beckoned to him. 'Now, right away. Quick, get your coat, it's late already.'

She was becoming more and more of a mystery to him. He did not know what to think of her to avoid being overwhelmed by the heights to which she rose, or astonished at the depths to which she could sink. He felt a dull, suppressed rage at this woman, whom he loved and with whom he had to struggle to stop her deceiving him with her lies. Who was she, and what did she want with him? What was she after? Why did she evade his ardent, impassioned declarations, but then look at him in a way that brought the pulse in his throat to a halt and sent icy shivers down his spine. Was she a penitent or a whore? Why had she suddenly come with him to this place in the middle of the night? Did she lust after thrills, did she want to whip her ageing blood into a frenzy and immerse herself in illusion? Or was she too faint-hearted for vice, and wanted to get drunk on the mere sight of it?

He thought of her white, transparent hands, which had so much goodness and wisdom in them, and among the pale fingers of which a painful sensuality grew like a red flower. He was overcome with a cruel determination to subdue this woman, to make her his, sooner or later.

Regina was still dancing with Valentin. She lay in his arms, abandoned, powerless, her lips twisted. Countless times now they had passed the piano, and every time Valentin threw a coin into the plate. He could have danced away all the money he possessed. His deep, burning eyes were wide open, hot and sure of victory. His grim, savage head was bent forward, and he felt Regina's breath on his face. His broad chest rose up, a strange gurgling sound choked in his lungs. He grasped the Countess brutally with both hands and pressed her helpless, twitching body against his. He led her into the most crowded part of the dance floor and thrust his knee between her thighs

41

as the wild keyboard in the corner jangled and set off on the tune once more.

Gradually the others could dance no more and sank onto the benches, panting. But the musician, dazed by Valentin's money, went on playing. The crowd on the dance-floor thinned. Many couples dropped to the ground and lay there, as if unconscious. The music washed over them in raucous waves.

On – keep going – again – the waltz – keep playing the waltz!

There is only one single couple flying round the wide, gaping dance hall. The others are leaning against the walls, drunkenly looking on as Countess Regina spins round with Valentin in a mad, obscene whirl, covered in sweat, unconscious, as if delirious.

Then the wild keyboard gives a sudden scream of despair and falls silent. A last, long, groaning note rises to the ceiling, then all is quiet. In the middle of the room Valentin and Countess Regina have collapsed to the smoky, dusty floorboards. The Countess is lying on her back, long and pale, like a corpse, her arms stretched out motionless alongside her body. On top of her, face downwards, lies Valentin, a stream of black, foaming blood pouring from his mouth through her dress to her soft, yellow skin, waking her from her swoon.

Hasty, rough hands carried her out into the darkness, trying to help.

But Regina sent them away. Undoing her dress, she let his blood run down into her hot silk chemise, and then she kissed him.

He opened his eyes and smiled. 'Do you love me, Countess?'

She kissed him and said, 'I suppose I must', and wiped the blood from his eyes with her silk chemise.

'And when will you be mine?' he whispered.

'Not yet . . . not yet, Valentin.'

At that the sick man's eyes darkened. 'At this moment Martha Bianca is lying in the Baron's bed. The whole town knows, and you know too. What more are you waiting for?'

The Countess went pale and trembled. Then she said softly, 'I am waiting until they're all finished. After Martha Bianca there will not be many more. I want to be the last, Valentin.'

Once more she kissed him on the lips then stood up. She pulled her dress together and ran out into the street. She ran quickly and straight ahead, as in a dream. Her lover's blood sticking to her skin like burning silk.

8

Since the evening when he had delivered up his mother to the hunchback, Joseph had been overcome with a profound sadness. His wild, unbridled soul had been shocked by what he had experienced that night and had fled in pain, leaving him alone, trembling and fearful in his empty, aimless life. And now he was like a timid child in the dark. It was not remorse that was tormenting him and making him feel unsure of himself, it was simply the grandiose image of that evil moment, rising up like a pillar from his drunkenness and dreams, giving him a sign from God. His hard, blind heart was heavy with the blood of shame.

He was the only person in the house whom Marietta did not avoid. That was the name of the blond girl from the village. She would talk to no one who came near her, not even to the cobbler. When sleep came upon her while she was praying, then she could talk to everyone, but by day she determinedly avoided them all, and if someone asked her a question, she would stare him in the face for a long time and not understand. But whenever she saw Joseph's pale, burning hands as he softly felt his way up the stairs and through the kitchen to his squalid room her lips would soften in a happy, friendly curve and she would go up to him trustingly and speak to him. The first time, he had tried to push his way past in sullen surprise, not answering, not even acknowledging her. Then he looked into her wide, shimmering eyes, boundlessly open to everything, and he stopped.

'You're ill, your lips are as white as a murderer's', she said to him.

'Your mouth is like honey . . .' he replied and could not go on. Her eyes held him and his voice dried up. All he could do was stand there and watch her go to her room.

After that day he often talked with her, in harsh, clipped words, hasty with secretiveness, so that the others would not hear what he was saying.

He became devout. Just as in the past the gypsy woman had knelt beside the cobbler, so he now knelt beside Marietta, looking at her as she prayed. Softly, humbly he came in through the door in the evening, as the service was beginning, looking no one in the face, hardly even aware that there was anyone else there apart from her. Only when his father's angry gaze fell on him would he give a start and bend his head lower over his clasped hands; he also turned away when Marietta looked towards him. Slowly, inexorably the radiance of the Lauretanian litany flooded his heart, blinding it, deafening it. That was the prayer, the long, deep, innermost prayer that Marietta had to say because it belonged to the Virgin Mary, because she was her servant and slave, and because she had seen her with her own eyes, the Queen in the grandeur of her bliss.

Like a wondrous, glowing song the words of the holy litany poured into the souls of those that were praying, into the souls of Marietta and Joseph, making their heads reel. As if in a delirium he repeated the words that all those around him were shouting out at the window-panes in vehement monotones, in fervent terror.

Behind the white curtain he could see the stars in the evening sky, pale and quivering and yet like the points of a huge, comforting diadem. He raised his hands and stammered,

'Pray for us.

Pray for us.'

He felt a wave of song surging through him that evening. He heard Marietta's voice beside him and he could tell from the tearful, ringing tones of her voice that that very evening he would drink the kisses of her lips like new wine. 'Your lips are red as honey', he had once said to her. Like wild honey, he thought, which the bees gather in the woods and to which the wind and the sun and the rain add their scent. He listened to the sound of her prayer and heard how she kept losing herself in the golden magic of their love, as in a miracle, how she immersed herself in it, as in a pool. Marietta fell into her hot, visionary sleep and her head sank onto Joseph's shoulder. Her hand almost broke his in a wild, all-consuming spasm of ecstasy as she saw the face of the Virgin Mary framed in the wood of the window-surround. Joseph looked into Marietta's eyes, which seemed to be wandering through a golden forest far away. Her poor, chapped lips went on speaking. Her words came through a veil, by fits and starts, as if in a transport of happiness:

'O spiritual rose . . .

O kindly Virgin . . .

O faithful virgin . . .'

And the response came stumbling out timidly in a hoarse chorus, tormented by wearisome labour, crushed by anxiety:

'Pray for us!

Pray for us!'

Marietta's hand crept up inside Joseph's sleeve and her white nails feverishly dug into the bare flesh of his arm. From time to time he too, when he closed his eyes and listened, when he prayed with the others in the dark, was almost swept up in the vision. Then his former life vanished like a dream and the surging wave of the Lauretanian litany carried him off into a beautiful silvery landscape. Outside the window, where only a short time ago the Virgin Mary with her crown had been, was a swaying hammock, and inside, stretched out on the floor in her thin blue dress, narrow hoops of metal with rubies burning in them round her bare legs, Marietta was looking at him, him alone, and her eyes wandered hither and thither in his, as in a golden forest.

Again he heard her ecstatic, high, ringing voice:

'O Ark of the Covenant –

O Tower of David –

O Ivory Tower –'

And then he heard her voice crack and start to fall and clearly, quite clearly and slowly break:

'O Morning Star –

O Golden House –'

'Have mercy on us!' Joseph cried out, so that the prayers of the others suddenly fell silent, and everything was still in the room in the cobbler's house. Then they all looked on in amazement and horror as Joseph held the blond girl in his arms and kissed her lips again and again. Marietta, their fair-haired saint, was lying in his lap, pale and smiling. She ran her thin hand through his shaggy mane and stroked it.

'Have mercy on us!' said Joseph once again, and kissed her.

Then he stood up, took Marietta's small body in his arms and carried her out through the door. Her flaxen hair was hanging across his body like a sash and her hand was feeling for the bare skin of his chest.

They all stood there, numb with shock, none daring to say a word. Then the door closed behind the pair. Joseph and Marietta were in the dark.

The stars were gathered together in a cluster of gold, forming a backdrop to the wide street. Since they did not know where they should go, they turned towards the stars, gradually coming closer to them. They walked side by side, holding hands like children. And as Marietta started coming to herself again, she asked Joseph what all this was, she no longer recognised her heart, and wasn't that the Virgin Mary over there by the golden stars.

Although he hardly understood it himself, Joseph explained to her that it was love and that it could change your heart and your life, just as she had changed his life.

She put her arms round his neck and looked at his mouth with the light of the Milky Way pouring over his face.

'How is it that your lips are not so ugly any more, not as white as a murderer's lips?'

And he kissed her, and it brought to mind the wild honey the bees make in the forest.

Then they continued their way down the road, towards the yellow cluster of stars. There were no more questions.

They never returned. Never.

9

Now there came evenings that touched the gables of the town with gentle, timid fingers and were sparing with the sun, which was swathed in red clouds. When the wind flew past Countess Regina's windows, it paused for a while, flitting through the twilight of the salon, looking for Martha Bianca's yellow hair and for her eyes. They were in the farthest, darkest, quietest corner, wide and shimmering, watching the clouds hide the sky behind silk and damask. Martha Bianca's eyes were like a door in a brightly lit room. They were not deep like the Countess', but they could remain steadfastly fixed for hours on a picture or a mouth, and they could shine with a wonderful radiance. It was like looking into a stream where there were little crowns with tiny points on the bed, as if someone had spilt some gold paint. Now they were fixed and shimmering, unable to tear themselves away from the clouds, staying with them almost the whole day. They did not blink when a hot tear welled up from the wide-open spaces of her heart far, far away and fell onto the carpet. Martha Bianca was crying. She was crying with a vehement, bewildered sadness that had found its way into her soul like a lost child, with an amazement beyond words that she did not shatter like a mirror. She could not tell how long she had been crying in this way. She was not conscious of her tears, she only felt them coming, laboriously, after a long journey, burning like hot stones blasting her throat.

Countess Regina walked past Martha Bianca's bitter dreams without saying a word, without touching them. But her soul had turned white as snow, white as the hair at her temples which the little mirror behind the curtain revealed to her when she sat at the window, shivering with cold. Her love for Valentin was tormenting her too and making her suffer. And the sight of her child's happiness seeping away with the tears that embroidered silver threads on the dark weave of the carpet brought great dismay, a tender, inexpressible sorrow into her life. She could not ask their cause; she knew Martha Bianca's soul, how shy and timid it was, how afraid. She knew she must be there when the pale face with the wide, helpless eyes beneath the yellow-gold hair became like a picture, earnest, without movement or joy. She knew she must be there and remain silent. She saw the darkness in her child's heart and was full of reproaches for the man who had blown out the candles that had burnt there with a devout and yearning flame. That was the young baron whom for a while she had almost loved because he had managed to bring such an intoxication of happiness, such hot, oblivious laughter to Martha Bianca's eyes that at the beginning the girl had almost died from it. And to die of happiness when it had become too great, too wild and painful for the body, when it killed the soul and consumed the heart like a dry rag, that must be the most beautiful death on earth – that had been often and long in the Countess' thoughts as she had watched Martha Bianca's cheeks grow white and transparent like a candle-flame, as she saw her hair grow dull and pale and dry in a fever of bliss. She knew everything, yes, she almost knew how it had come about between the Baron and her child. Valentin must have told her a hundred times when she lay in his arms, full of fear at this alien love. He kept on talking of it, between kisses and the lascivious bites which he inflicted on her body with cruel teeth, because he saw how it tormented her. Now there was grief and resentment in her against the young robber who had taken Martha Bianca's life in his hands like a chess piece, dragging the love out of her child's soul with his bold and dangerous mouth, torturing that love and hurting it. God only knew what he was doing with it! It was a long time now since she had heard anything of the two of them, she had become solitary, cut off from the world, no one came to the red drawing room any longer, neither Daniel Jesus, nor Baron Sterben himself, nor anyone else. Only Valentin came, every day to her room, her knees started trembling at the mere sound of his steps outside the door. He was vicious and violent. He hit her with his big bony hands so that her delicate yellow skin was covered in bruises and she had to clamp her teeth together so as not to cry out loud. But she could no longer escape him, he was her master, she knelt at his feet and begged for mercy. Then he would raise her up to him, pull back her head and kiss her so that all at once she forgot everything, her tongue hung in her throat, heavy and sizzling like red-hot iron, her consciousness disintegrated like a house of cards and she sank to the floor with a moaning cry.

Valentin knew nothing about Martha Bianca and the Baron either. Their love had grown daily more secret, more hidden. The Countess was left in mute dismay, facing a mystery the solution to which she awaited with anxiety. For seven days now Bianca's tears had been falling onto the carpet with the fantastic design and dark colours that covered the drawing-room floor with its marvel. They were becoming hotter and hotter, more and more sorrowful. They shone so brightly with blood and sadness that at times they fell like rare, beautiful, crimson gems. For a week now her eyes, wide and shimmering in the darkness at the back of the room, had been staring fixedly at the clouds outside, her hands trembling like the garden leaves in the wind. In bitter apprehension her concern for her child grew. Worry made her ill and ugly, her movements old. Every tear that Martha Bianca wept etched another line round her mouth.

It was towards the end of May when Martha Bianca was wakened once more by the moon, which came into her room with the scent of a tree in blossom. There was a bright, silver light, and Martha Bianca had been dreaming of the evening when she had run through the streets in her nightdress and cloak, barefoot, to find her lover's house. She had opened her eyes to see the figure of her mother kneeling and praying at her bedside. The moonlight was flickering on her white hair and on the pale face in which she could see the thousand sorrows, the bitterness and fear that had crossed it since she had last looked at it. That had been a few days ago, before she had started staring at the red clouds. A wild, expansive longing came into Martha Bianca's heart. She threw her arms round the Countess' beautiful neck, which had a nasty, bloody scratch running across it, kissed the hands which were trying to pray for her and the mouth which had grown so ugly within a few hours, and wept for the hundredth time those great, shimmering tears in which her sadness and her blood, her poor, betrayed love and her generous, unstinting heart gathered together, entwining like a posy in the light of the moon. Then she told the Countess everything.

Baron Sterben was dead. He had died in the arms of the gypsy girl, Hagar. Since the cobbler had kicked her out of his house she had not gone back, but had returned to the Baron. He had kept her hidden from Martha Bianca, and while he was sealing her childish lips with flimsy lies and his hands were caressing her amber hair, the gypsy girl was in the next room, waiting for the moment when he would turn again to her body and its greedy lusts. He had forbidden Hagar to show herself when Martha Bianca was with him and had cut off her defiant protests with a look which silenced her at once. Thus he had deceived Martha Bianca for weeks, while her great, simple heart had believed him, turning a joyful red like the bushes blossoming against the wall in the Baron's garden. Until one day she found herself staring into his dead eyes. Then she knew everything. He was lying in bed. The gypsy girl was lying beside him, her eyes stopped like a clock from the nameless horror.

Martha Bianca had come an hour earlier than usual and had gone straight in, as she always did. On his face she could still see the raptures of love from which he had died. His delicate, febrile heart had collapsed in the wild frenzy, amid the kisses and cries, the lust and passion of the young gypsy girl, who had killed him with her lean body just as surely as if she had cut his throat. Love had burst his heart open and torn his soul apart like a piece of cloth. The gypsy girl was kneeling beside him in the bed. Her nightdress has slipped down, revealing her small, dangerous breasts. She was kneeling beside his corpse, mute. Giddy with horror, she looked across at Martha Bianca who, her face petal-white, walked up to her lover's bed and looked into his lifeless eyes. The rapturous intoxication which stared out at her from them, glassy and dulled though it was in the moment of death, was like a flame burning up her heart in red-hot grief. Her childhood was suddenly at an end. She knew and understood everything. Her love had been a dream, a lie from the very start. The man before her had died from another's love. Fairy tales did not come true. Magic was an illusion. He had played with her as if she were a smile he had met by chance. Because she had eyes like shining globes and amber hair. He had taken her soul and her thirteen-year-old body, which had almost been shattered by the joy, as his heart had been by the gypsy's love. But he had found room for another's eyes and another's kisses, whilst her life had been filled to overflowing with his. Beside her heart he had found room for another's passion, violent, consuming, blind, and for which he had died without a thought for Bianca, far from her and filled to the brim with the bubbling enjoyment of another's moment in which he had drowned. Martha Bianca was ashamed. She was ashamed because she had been his lover. She was ashamed because she had given herself, her whole life, to him for whom she had been no more than a toy, a brief, smiling, amorous caprice.

Now she could see clearly. Her love was blown away like dandelion seeds in the late-summer storms. But it left the poison of sadness in her soul, that great, never-ending sadness which only comes once in our lives, when our best days are gone, never to return. For a long time her gaze rested on the gypsy girl, who was kneeling beside the Baron's corpse, still in the grip of horror. Then she turned away and went home. Her heart was withered, her soul in distress. She wept, and her tears were as endless as her sorrow. She was filled with shame and remorse.

Thus it was that in that night Martha Bianca told her mother the story of her love. The Countess listened, wide-eyed and with twitching lips. In her isolation she had not heard that Baron Sterben had died. She was deeply affected by the story of his death. It made her think of Valentin and herself, and she felt the fragrant nocturnal light caressing the scar on her neck. That was the way love had always been, from the very beginning, ever since she had known it, tears and wounds, sadness and cruelty. Then she took her child's head in her beautiful white hands, the fingers of which crackled with a rich sensuality, and covered the scar on her neck with Martha Bianca's hair and tears. They wept together on that spring night and held hands and wept until the moon turned pale silver and disappeared, until down in the garden a bird began to warble sleepily of the roses of summer.

10

Anton was lying on his bed staring into the blackness. His face was like a pale mask in the dark. In his soul there was something immense and strange, something ponderous and terrible going round and round in circles like a hobbled animal, and he could not tell what it was. His eyes were searching. They pierced the ceiling, the walls and floors, they looked inside himself until they were weary and his lids started to sting. They found nothing. It was all in vain, finished. How had it come about that now he was alone, that he could not get the thought out of his mind that once he had sought God and now he could not even pray? His hands had gone dry from fear of the evil around him so that he could not put them together in the sight of Grace. Where was God? Where was the kingdom that he had dreamt up in long, tangled prayers when people came and brought their shattered faith to him? Where was Margaret, his wife?

It was a week ago now that Margaret had left the house, suddenly and secretly, like a conversation stopping all at once. Anton knew that she would never return. He stared red-eyed into the night, and things and people grew terrible in his heart. At times they were like glass behind which he could see their longing with its violent, twisted fingers rattling and pounding at the glass walls until they were covered in blood and pus.

Then the cobbler was overcome with an insane, uncontrollable fear. The sweat froze in white patches on the skin of his face, spread like a terrible leprosy over his arms. His mind was blank. He had forgotten everything and was filled with unspeakable dread alone in the darkness, dread of his God and of his wife's sin, which rose up before him like an immense, terrifying, leafless, tree. The matches trembled in his huge hand as he lit the candle and examined his severe, haggard face in the mirror. He wanted to remind himself of his eyes, which in prayer had so often been like two bright candles, of his faith and of himself. Framed in the mirror he found a pale, alien face with deep shadows and furrows, which he could neither explain nor understand. He searched his memory for a hymn or a verse from the Bible which would help him bear his loneliness, but he could remember nothing. Everything had been obliterated by a secret, perfidious iniquity which was like a dark pillar concealing everything he had once loved. Since his son Joseph had vanished, heading for the stars at the end of the street with Marietta, his house had been deserted, no one came to pray any more as they used to. A mysterious, alien power had scattered his empire and left his belief as full of holes as a sieve. It had branded his wife's soul with poisoned pincers, so that she had fled from her own wounds, from the spasms and dread of her own lust to a place where Sin would throw its red cloak over her, so that she would no longer feel shame at herself and at the humility she stole from God, like a whore, to throw it away perhaps on someone who would spit on it and crush her last scrap of dignity beneath his foot.

As if in a daze, Anton pressed his fists against his face and asked, as he had asked before, trembling in fear and sorrow, where was the enemy? Where was the prophet the girl had spoken of in her trance, when she had been overcome with holy sleep so that she spoke like the Virgin herself, whom she saw in her dreams in her own room and whom she loved as he had loved his God when he had still been able to pray and his wife had still been with him?

'There will be no one who will not bow before him. Not even you! Not even you!'

Thus Marietta's sleep had spoken to him, and now he knew that the words would be fulfilled.

He lay stretched out on the floor, digging his fingers into the decaying flesh of the boards. His face beat against the floor as if in madness, and a voice kept on crying within him, 'Where is the enemy? Where is the enemy? For the love of God, where is he?'

Suddenly the gypsy girl was standing before the cobbler in the half-opened door. She had crept up noiselessly in the dark and was looking at him with dull, smouldering eyes. She stood there like a slim, motionless stone, not making the least movement.

Anton raised his head and recognised her, tears and astonishment in his eyes. A painful, cowardly horror crept over his gigantic frame and in a flicker of fear he saw, as in a vision, the day when he had kicked out at her because he had looked into her bright, hungry eyes and could suddenly read them like an open book. The enemy! The enemy! was the cry that had echoed round his mind, but now he knew that she was not the enemy. The gypsy girl was merely a messenger, a puzzle set by the outsider, the illusionist who had taken away his empire, a puzzle he used to trick men and deceive them. Who could he be? The gypsy girl knew. He would ask her.

He stood up and turned his ravaged face to Hagar, who stood there unmoving in a long dress that reached from her neck to the ground. And before he could ask she told him everything in a few words, every one like a cracked glass:

'Anton, your wife is in Villa Jesus, in bed with the rich hunchback, kissing his hump as if it were a crucifix. She has wound her hair round her head like a crown. Daniel is laughing; this evening he is giving a party for her in the villa.'

The cobbler turned pale as a corpse. In his broad face only his lips were a burning red. His great heart stood still, then he raised his hands, threw his head back and screamed, again and again. It must have been twenty times he screamed at the ceiling the one name he had feared and which was now a black menace stuck to his heart: the prophet . . . the prophet:

'Daniel Jesus!'

Exhausted and blind with blood and horror, he fell at the gypsy girl's feet, filled with a strange aching which consumed him, which sucked all the yearning out of him and left his throat as bitter as decay. He could feel the gypsy girl's hands on his neck, could hear her breath singeing his hair. He was like a wall which a storm had blown apart, a door someone had pushed open for sin. Once more he pulled himself up and thrust her back into the darkness. She had slipped her dress off her shoulders and was standing there, naked but for her shoes and stockings. She crept up to him like a cat. He turned his face away and tried to keep her from him with his arms. She undid his shirt, and when the cobbler felt her hot, lascivious tongue on his chest, when her spittle ran down his skin in scorching trails, his hand fell to the ground like a lump of iron, and he did not resist as the gypsy girl devastated the huge body she had lusted after for so long, like hail flattening a field of corn.

11

The Villa Jesus was outside the town. Its narrow windows were shining almost white in the warm night, which blew a fragrant trickle of wind through the blossoming trees, beside which the slender Renaissance columns looked like women's bare arms. The fountain, which could be seen through the bars of the gate, was chattering all the time, sometimes giving a sly chuckle and keeping up a stream of nonsensical, ironic remarks. At times, in a fit of high spirits, it would send its beautiful, bright water splashing all over the lilacs and giggle quietly. The garden was surrounded by a high wall, amazingly high almost. The wind got caught in the corners, as in a seashell, and scurried about among the smooth sanded paths which shone in the light from the villa windows like a net of gold.

The gate was ajar and Martha Bianca was standing outside, hesitating. She had been driven here by a timid, moody fear. She knew that Daniel had been waiting at the town gates with his carriage that evening to take her mother and Valentin to the Villa Jesus. Now the night was almost over and the Countess had still not returned. Bianca had been so tormented by her trembling love that she was unable to sleep and bewildering, nightmarish, half-waking dreams had come to frighten her. She had shrouded her body in a loose, clinging housecoat and hurried out of the town, along the dusty road until she came to the gates of the villa. Now she was standing there looking across at the windows, from which the wind was scattering the disjointed notes of a violin, laughter and cries over the lawn and throwing them into the astonished fountain. The revels were not yet over, the warm air of the garden was filled with the sweet, overpowering scent of dark, heavy wines, over which the fragrance of champagne floated like a bubbling cloud. With slow steps Martha Bianca went up to the entrance. She wanted to go to her mother, to ask her not to be angry with her. She could not help it if she was too frightened when she was alone at home and had no one to kiss the pallor from her lips and take her long hair in her hands, as her mother always did. She would not be angry because she had followed her, she would not punish her. It was dark and she was all alone.

By one of the doors two servants tied a mask over her eyes. Carnival in spring, thought Martha Bianca, opening the door into the ballroom, from which came the enticing strains of jubilant dance music, yearning and wonderful, lively and dreamy, like coloured pearls running down from the violinist's bow to the floor, sorrowful and rapturous, love songs burning with flames of desire and devotion, songs as sweet as a woman's kisses. She was plunged into bright light. She had to close her eyes and, dazzled, felt for the wall with her hands. When she opened them again she saw the huge, silvery room with flowers and candles, with shimmering glass beads on the chandeliers and coloured crystals in front of the flames. The band was hidden behind a curtain and the music seemed like a magic spell. In the middle of the room Daniel Jesus was sitting on a scarlet throne beside a massive, naked woman who had wound her hair round her head like a crown and was looking at the hunchback with shining eyes. Round them the people were dancing with that wild, feverish intoxication that the music laid on their hearts, that came over their blood as they danced, as heavy and red as love. All the women wore a mask and were naked like the tall woman on the throne in the middle. The bright light from the thousand candles glittered on the white skin, which had grown moist and matt in the course of the night of dissipation, like the opal gleaming in the earring of the Countess whom Martha Bianca's eye had now found among the throng on the dance floor. There was a long, watery blue veil fluttering round her body which, in its yellow glow, contrasted strangely with the milky white of the others. The gauzy material was held together at the neck by a gold ring, just at the point where the red scar ran like a cut across the dark, throbbing vein. Valentin was dancing with the Countess and his bony hands had torn great holes in her veil, so that she hung on his arms with naked breasts and naked thighs, just like the other women, whom Martha Bianca did not recognise.

A brown, supple body glided across the room, steely muscles on its lean limbs, slim and tough as a cat. The gypsy girl. She slipped through the quivering women and their partners' stuttering lust to the window, which stood ajar. She pushed it open and whistled. From outside came the scrape of mortar on the cobbler's heavy shoes as he clambered up, holding onto the window-ledge with both hands. His face rose over the edge, wild and deathly pale, and his eyes looked round the ballroom.

'Can you see your wife beside Daniel Jesus? Can you see his fingers on her hot flesh, her mouth opening with delight?'

The cobbler's eyes widened, as deep and empty as a dark pit. So dark that all at once the candles in the chandelier and sconces guttered. The gypsy girl knelt before him and whispered, her tongue flickering in and out, 'Can you see your wife, Master Anton? Can you see your wife?'

Martha Bianca was still leaning by the door, watching. Suddenly she no longer understood this night. Her soul was filled with dread, a sheer spurt of terror at the sight of Daniel Jesus and the woman with the massive body sitting beside him on the scarlet throne, her hair wound round her head like a crown. She felt a rush of fear at the gleam in the eyes of the women flying past her, at the music which never stopped playing, at her mother, dancing naked with a hundred others. She was about to go and ask her to come home with her when she felt four hands holding her back. She turned round and saw two lackeys who were pointing at her clothes and jerking their heads. They were mutes, incapable of speech. But Martha Bianca understood them. Her face turned as pale as the love that had once been in her heart, many days ago. Slowly she unbuttoned her dress at the neck and shoulders, then stood there, as naked as the rest.

'A child!' she heard a voice cry out in astonishment.

The dancers drew back, astounded, forming a passage along

which Martha Bianca walked towards her mother. The women stopped dancing and looked at her in amazement. Martha Bianca was beautiful. Her amber hair was like a stream flowing down her silver back, her skin was as white as birchbark. In the harsh light of the crystal chandelier the nipples on her little breasts glittered like two wounds. Her eyes were wide and full of humility as she knelt at her mother's feet and looked up at her. The Countess was jolted out of her trance. Bewildered and moved, she sought the closeness to her daughter she had felt in the night when Martha Bianca had made her confession. She stood there, trembling.

Then Valentin lifted the kneeling child up off the floor in his two hands and said with a laugh, 'Come and dance, Martha Bianca.'

Martha Bianca looked up at him and saw the same glow in his eyes that she had seen before. She had often seen it in Baron Sterben's eyes. Baron Sterben was dead. How could it be? How could another man have inherited his eyes? Baron Sterben was dead. She had loved him very much, she had done everything for his sake, for his eyes, for these eyes which she now saw again.

The Countess was still standing there, silent and trembling. Her veil was torn, Martha Bianca could see the scar on her neck. She took a step closer, looked at Valentin, at his cruel hands, then she said softly, haltingly, absently, as if in her sleep, 'Mother – who – did – that – to – you?'

A shudder passed over the Countess' features. Her wide, startled eyes looked across at Valentin. He had placed his hands round Bianca's waist and kept on feverishly repeating the same words, 'Come and dance with me, Martha Bianca.'

Then a shrill trumpet somewhere in the room sounded a commanding fanfare and Martha Bianca saw Daniel Jesus and the massive woman rise from their seat and two mute lackeys carry in a black crown, the precious stones in it as deathly pale as tears. Daniel Jesus took the black circlet and placed it on his huge, grotesque head. The band began to play to a wild, hustling beat. A light snapped in Valentin's eyes.

Martha Bianca stood there, white as a flame. She could see

Valentin's face, could see the Countess' scar, the crown Daniel was wearing, and the two lackeys whose tongues he had cut out so they would remain mute for the rest of their days. A great, mind-wrenching horror fell on her heart. Without knowing why, her thoughts turned to Baron Sterben and the dead Valeska. In her sudden dread, she gave a long, high-pitched scream that made everyone look up. The room fell so quiet one could hear the tinkling of the glass crystals in the metal chandeliers on the ceiling. She cast one last desperate, tremulous look of love at her mother's staring eyes, then screamed once more and fled like a madwoman from the room, past the women's naked breasts, past Margaret's massive body, beside which the black crown was like a viper wound painfully round Daniel's head.

She ran. She ran down the steps into the garden, naked and with the black mask over her eyes. She kept on running, running away in horror. On the lawn below the windows the gypsy girl was lying like a doll, a smile on her face, her eyes blank with madness, looking up at the big acacia which thrust a thick, blossoming branch into the widow by which she had been kneeling an hour ago, whispering to the cobbler.

Anton? The cobbler? Where could he be? The gypsy girl smiled, her lips hot and strangely twisted. Brightly coloured, long-forgotten dreams floated past her soul, like goldfish by the bulbous glass of their bowl, their fins glittering in the water and jingling with a prink . . . prink . . . prink.

The gypsy girl smiled. An astonished smile, guileless as a child's. She was happy because she could not remember anything any longer. The reason she was smiling was because Anton, the cobbler, who had hung himself with her belt up in the acacia tree, had goggle eyes and a wide-open mouth like the golden fishes in their bowl . . . prink . . . prink . . . you look as white as a dead man, Anton, and I love you. –

The street beside the Villa Jesus, from which you could hear the fountain teasing the lilac bush, was completely filled with moonlight and stars. From a tiny, far-off cloud the wind blew some warm rain into the light. Silvery white as a birch tree, her yellow hair falling over her eyes and the black mask on her face, Martha Bianca was running, her heart full of horror and love. She was running in an unknown direction, away from the town, farther and farther, and the blood from her lacerated feet was like coral on the cobblestones.

SEVERIN'S ROAD INTO DARKNESS

Book One
One Year in Severin's Life

1

That autumn Severin was twenty-three. In the afternoons, when he came home, drained from the drudgery of office work, he would throw himself onto the black leather sofa in his room and sleep until the evening. Not until the street-lights were lit would he go out. Only during the long, scorching days of summer did he see the sun as he made his way round the city; or on Sundays, when the whole day was his own and his wanderings took him back to his brief student days.

Severin had abandoned his studies after two or three semesters and taken a position. Now he spent his mornings sitting in the loathsome office, his pasty, adolescent and still beardless face bent over columns of figures. As the chill in the room crept up his limbs, he could feel an unhealthy, febrile discontent taking hold of him, arousing his restlessness. The monotonous sameness of the days made his hands tremble. A leaden weariness gnawed at his temples and he pressed his eyeballs back into his skull until they hurt.

For one whole rainy October week now he had not seen Zdenka. With an angry sweep of the arm he pushed the letters in which she daily begged him to come and see her to one side and left them unanswered. Desires which Zdenka could not satisfy were beginning to make their presence felt in the dull throbbing of his blood. And when he went out in the evening, still dazed from sleep, it was always the same; he was overcome with a tense feeling of expectation, a confused and bizarre curiosity. His wide-eyed gaze was drawn toward the city where the people moved like shadows on a screen. The noise of the cars, the clatter of the trams merged with the people's voices into a harmonious effervescence of sound from which, now and then, a single call or cry would ring out, and he would listen to it die away with a tense alertness, as if he had just missed something special. Most of all he liked the streets that were hidden from the bustle of the city centre. If he screwed up his eyes and looked through his half-closed lids the houses took on a fantastic appearance. He walked along the walls of the large gardens at the back of hospitals and institutes, his nostrils filled with the smell of rotting leaves and damp earth. Somewhere nearby there was a church, he knew. Early in the evening it was already deserted here and only a few people came. Severin stood in the shadow of the projecting upper stories and wondered what it was that was making his heart pound.

Was it this city with its dark façades, its wide squares filled with silence, its withered passion? He kept feeling as if invisible hands were brushing against him. He remembered that even by day he often found himself walking round a long-familiar district as if it were new to him. On Sunday mornings he sometimes went past the hospital and the Karlov church down Na slupi to the low-lying part of the city. He was filled with amazement at the thought that he had been living here since his childhood. When the sunshine gleamed on the crumbling steps, the image of the winter evenings here with the snow gusting through the streets and the lamps glittering in the muddy puddles forced its way into his mind. He felt as if he were in the grip of a magic spell. The urge to break the spell and turn it against someone else grew within him.

His own barrenness often brought him to the brink of despair. He was full of a bitterness that squandered its strength in futile curses, and of a lassitude that craved perverse pleasures. Of all this Zdenka was completely unaware. And now, with upturned coat-collar and lips pressed together in a sullen line, he was making his meandering way through the city toward the Moldau, where she was expecting him.

For years the long, busy street he was going down had been his route to school. Here, on his way home, he had smoked his first cigarettes, here they had discussed tactics for the great battles with the Czech boys that were fought out on the ramparts of Vinohrady. He had never distinguished himself as a great leader or hero in them, but he had never allowed his cowardice to show either. Standing up to the stones thrown by their enemies gave him a secret sensual thrill. In these battles all the tales of knights and bold seafarers that he read at home awoke to a flickering but none-the-less real life that brought a flush to his cheeks, a sweaty moistness to the palms of his hands, and made him catch his breath with suppressed excitement. Since that time there had been no experience to match it in intensity throughout his adolescence. But with the years the blind urge which had driven him out to join in the schoolboy brawls on the deserted ramparts had grown and grown until he could feel it choking him. Sometimes he was seized with a senseless fear, a horror that this was all there was to his life. Since he had grown up and begun to earn his living, blank, bare walls had risen around him, blocking his view. Everywhere he looked he was surrounded by the stupefying routine of the everyday world. In the morning he went to the office and at midday he came home; he slept through the rest of the daylight hours. He felt like someone standing in a pit: however fast he shovelled out the earth, the fine, shifting sand kept on trickling back down, filling up the hole.

As a child he had once possessed a book which stuck in his mind ever afterwards. It was the first volume of a novel about the Hussite wars. The second volume was missing and Severin made no attempt to find it. He preferred the book as it was, ending in the middle of great events. There were gypsies in it who had a robbers' den among the crags of the Devil's Wall by Vyšší Brod, fierce mercenaries who diced for the women in the taverns, moonlit nights in which people dug for the mandrake root in the forest. There was an enchanted garden where misshapen dwarves mocked travellers who had lost their way, where magic caves opened up and iron lions sank rattling into the ground when someone approached. The comet dragged its blood-red tail across the sky, and in Bohemia there was war. Severin was thinking about the book as he went to meet Zdenka.

In the park in Charles Square everything was quiet. There were just a few courting couples whispering among the bushes. As he walked Severin kicked the withered leaves on the paths. The street lamps were already lit, hanging over the trees like moons. Severin peered through the light at the first stars. He was in the grip of a morose restlessness which kept pulling him back into the park while Zdenka was already waiting for him. He took off his hat and felt the dampness of the evening on his hair. The clock on the tower of the law courts sounded, the strokes slowly echoing through the branches. Severin listened to them with bitterness in his heart. In his soul he felt the feeble flicker of an impotent craving for a turbulent and colourful existence, such as was described in the book. It flared up into a devouring flame, glowing with the vision of a monstrous and brutal life. Beyond the confines of Charles Square he could sense the city.

Severin left the twilight of the park and set off down the first street he came to. Again he immersed himself in the noise, registering individual voices. And somewhere at the back of his mind it began to dawn on him that it was people who made up life; that it was from the interplay with them that everything came which he felt would give his life richness, meaning, thrill; comet-riven nights and devastation and the heart's enigmas. With an exquisite shock he remembered the evening when he had gone with a friend to see a play at a theatre in a Czech quarter. He had never been particularly discriminating as far as that kind of thing was concerned. The wheedling sentimentality with which the actors courted their audience of petty-bourgeois philistines was just the spur his senses needed. More than elsewhere, there, amid the rantings of histrionic actors and the tears and laughter of crudely made-up women he had felt the hot and uncouth desires of his soul. His attention had been aroused by a girl who moved the audience to tears with her disappointment in love. There was something in the way she stretched her thin body, in the line of her shoulders and neck which reminded him of Zdenka. Afterwards, although he did not admit it openly to himself, his emotions had been in a strange state of turmoil, the same feeling that always seized him when he listened to the embarrassed silence during the pauses between music in the all-night cafés or when he loitered, tense and hesitant, in the evening on street corners. It was the feeling that there was something near him, something so strong, so physical, that it made the air quiver, which he felt for with his hands, but could never quite touch.

Then came the glare of the lights of Ferdinandstrasse and the brightness of the shop windows dazzled him. It was already getting late and he hurried. He saw Zdenka standing outside the National Theatre, her sweet face smiling a greeting at him from among the crowd.

2

That was also the autumn when Severin got to know Lazarus Kain. He had a shop at the top of Stephansgasse, not far from the large botanical gardens. A few volumes in worn cloth bindings and yellowing brochures in foxed covers under the glass of the display case indicated to passers-by that this was a bookshop. Over the door, on a sign regularly washed by rain and snow, stood in faded letters the name of the owner with, below it, the words 'Antiquarian Bookseller'.

The shop was narrow and low, and even by day it was lit by a gas light. But in winter it could be very cosy when the iron stove in the corner almost glowed red with zeal and Lazarus sat at his desk leafing through massive catalogues or teaching tricks to Anton, his pet raven. During the holidays and in the early autumn business was slack, and old Lazarus usually left his daughter in charge of the shop to rove the surrounding district. He pattered up and down the lane with his short steps, peering up at the upper storeys of the houses. He was some-what short-sighted, and the gaslight in his dark shop had further weakened his eyes. He watched the servant-girls as they leant their firm breasts on the window-ledges to shake out their dusters over the street. He screwed up his eyes and the blood rushed to his yellow cheeks. Or he would stand by St. Adalbert's column, his eyes following the wet-nurses from the nearby maternity home. Not far away was the grubby tavern popularly known as 'Poison Inn'. Lazarus Kain remembered the days when medics used to gather there to spend the evenings dancing with the midwives. He sometimes used to go there himself and sit in a corner watching the goings-on. Now the inn had a new owner and was almost completely deserted by day. The only customers were a few Czech youths playing at skittles in the neglected garden where a surly waitress brought them their beer in cracked glasses.

He also often used to sit in the little Pilsner Bar opposite St.

Stephen's. Business was not very lively there either on the summer mornings when he visited it. It was only later that the priests from the nearby deanery would arrive for their lunch. Lazarus would sit in the window-seat, peering through the green curtain and admiring the slim ankles of the girls hurrying past. He was close on fifty, but women were still his great passion. At home, on the top shelves in his bookshop, were the choice volumes he kept for connoisseurs and his best customers: dangerous and flagrant books, privately printed editions from France and Germany, copper engravings, rare translations from the time of Rétif de la Bretonne. He felt a lover's tenderness for these treasures, which he would take down again and again to gloat over, stroking them with his thin fingers. He was reluctant to part with them, even at the high prices they commanded. His regret when he saw them in the hands of their purchasers was genuine, and he felt as if they were carrying off some long-cherished item of personal property from his house. There were only two creatures he loved more than these books, his raven Anton, an old and somewhat bedraggled bird which had kept him company in the bookshop for years, and his daughter Susanna.

It was in the little inn opposite the church that Severin made Lazarus Kain's acquaintance. Outside, the church bells were ringing for Sunday mass and the two of them were gazing at the young women who, deep in thought, prayerbooks in their hands, walked past the tavern window. Lazarus pushed his glass across the table closer to Severin's and began to talk. As he spoke, movement came into his withered face and under the close-cropped whiskers his cheeks flushed. He talked of the cold and unimaginative character of the modern age in which the lust for money had killed off the enjoyment of all other passions. With half-closed lids, behind which his eyes had the feverish glint of private pleasure, he started describing his favourite period, eighteenth-century France. His stories of Louis XV's Parc-aux-Cerfs escapades were recounted with colour and zest, and a quiver of envious longing entered his voice when he told the rapt Severin about Madame Junus, the procuress of genius who had the ability to

73

amaze even the jaded Paris of those times with new and ingenious sensations.

Those days will never return, he said, with a note of genuine sadness in his voice. For a while they both sat in silence in the gloom of the tavern, musing on the erotic marvels of past ages, while the church bells across the street fell silent, leaving a golden resonance in the air which grew softer and fainter until finally it was inaudible. Severin stole a glance at the bald-pated Lazarus, who was once more looking out of the window, and scrutinised his Jewish profile, criss-crossed by thousands of tiny wrinkles. He suspected that this man suffered from the same malady as he did, an intense and unsatisfied desire which had sought refuge from a narrow and pointless life in old books . He was seized with pity for the old man, who for years had wasted his spirit on dead pictures. They talked for a little while longer, and Lazarus told Severin about his daughter and his raven. As he left he invited him to visit him in his shop.

A few days later Severin followed up the invitation. On a low upholstered chair beside the stove sat Susanna. The weather was still fine and the bookseller had not yet started to light the stove. In spite of that, once the sun went down a damp chill trickled into the houses in the narrow lane. Susanna had wrapped a black shawl round her shoulders and the gaslight was dancing on the pages of the book that lay open in her lap. With no signs of surprise, Lazarus stood up behind the counter and greeted Severin. His bald head gleamed in the light as he bent over a couple of rare and valuable tomes, examining them through his magnifying glass. Severin patiently listened to his explanations, glancing idly across at Susanna, who sat in silence reading her book. Her brown hair was brushed straight back and the shadows of her long lashes were dancing on her cheeks. Once, when she looked up, their eyes met.

After that Severin went to visit Lazarus Kain regularly. He could not get the image of the young Jewess out of his mind and it kept him awake at nights. Susanna was not what one would call a beauty, but there was a suspicious spark flickering in her eyes which stood in sharp contrast to the serenity of her lips. Deep within their velvety depths was a glow of telltale intensity which made Severin bashful and aroused his desire at the same time. He had sometimes seen the stars flicker like that when, drained from some unfathomable urge, he had looked up at the sky on his way home late at night. Severin sought out those eyes, through the smoke of his cigarette, over her father's bald, birdlike head and behind the brief flutterings of the raven, which hopped about from one corner of the cramped room to another as if it were in a cage. Susanna fixed them on him with an expression of inscrutable earnestness, never taking part in the conversation, never addressing a single word to him. When he spoke to her she replied with a few curt and listless phrases, which irritated him and made him give up the attempt to engage her in conversation. So he chatted to the bookseller and looked at the old lithographs and heliogravures he showed him.

One day, when Susanna happened not to be present, Lazarus promised to introduce him to Dr. Konrad. He made the suggestion hesitantly, as if it were the final cautious stage in taking him into his confidence. At Severin's bewildered question he told him about the huge studio in one of the new houses which had been built on the land from which the hovels of the old Jewish quarter had been cleared. With the remains of what had once been a considerable fortune Dr. Konrad had rented a painter's studio which was now used for quite different purposes. Potted palms and carpets gave the room an exotic air, while the only things to indicate the owner's profession were a couple of picture frames in one corner, an easel and a few sketches of heads turned to the wall. In fact it was a long time since Dr. Konrad had held a brush in his hand. He would spend hours lying on his comfortable Turkish sofa, rolling perfumed cigarettes by hand and drinking the French cognac and soda that his manservant brought. Or he listened to his mistress' lethargic twangings on her mandoline. She was a spoilt blonde who went by the name of Rušena. During the afternoons a swarm of guests came to visit him: young men-about-town in dinner jackets with grey spats over their patent-leather shoes; old roués in elegant suits, the ivory butt of their riding crops at their lips; artists with floppy hats and grubby collars; models in silk blouses and tight skirts passing their free time sipping the Doctor's sweet liqueurs; here and there, too, was the occasional society girl or woman, some shy and uncertain, others more brazen than necessary, but both drawn by the manifold attraction a life of dissolution exerts on outsiders. All that Lazarus told him, and the rest Severin guessed from the old man's repressed excitement and his restless hands.

As he went out into the street Susanna came towards him through the evening mist. She looked at him with a smile which made his whole body tremble, as if from an electric shock. Mechanically and without hesitation he took her hand. It felt warm.

'Come', Susanna said to him, the same smile still on her lips. He went back into the house with her. The light had not yet been lit on the stairs. He kissed her on the back of the neck, which her dress had left uncovered.

'Your father's in the shop', he said. Susanna merely nodded and led him up narrow stairways and along passages to her room.

3

It was on a clear, frosty evening the previous winter that Zdenka had fallen in love with Severin. The street had brought them together as they both wandered aimlessly among the hurrying people. The little stoves of the roast-chestnut sellers stood, like red-eyed locomotives, beside the pavement. Slowly, one by one, a few snowflakes tumbled into the light of the street-lamps. As Zdenka watched them, they brought back to mind the bright wings of the gnats flitting round the shining globes in summer. She was still lost in thought when Severin addressed her, but she gave a merry laugh and as she looked up into his pleasant, boyish face, burnished by the cold, she at once fell into a carefree, light-hearted mood. They walked round the city together, looking at the bright and cheerful displays in the toy-shop windows, where there was a little railway running on real rails, and admiring the stuffed tiger a carpet-dealer had put in his window. They stopped by the iced-over panes of the delicatessen with golden sprats gleaming in white wooden boxes. Then Severin bought something for their supper and she went with him to his bachelor flat.

Zdenka worked in an office until six. Her parents were both dead and she lived by herself in a room on the Old Town Square. During those unhappy years, when she had to make her own way through life, she had several times given herself to other men. She sobbed and kissed Severin as she begged his forgiveness for the fact that he was not the first man to whom she had given herself. He accepted her quivering tenderness as due tribute and later, when he realised that for her the impulse of that first evening was growing into a passion, he still treated her as casually as ever. She was a convenient pastime in the emptiness of his jaded heart, which stood firm amid the trusting radiance of her love. When she told him how happy she was, he listened to her lilting alto, amused at the naivety of her expression, but basically she left him cold. She had nothing of that consuming fire, that elemental incandescence his soul needed. She was a minor event, trifling and cloying, with nothing of the power of destiny, of no deeper interest to him.

For Zdenka, however, Severin was a miraculous experience. Ever since the moment when he had spoken to her in the street and then, an hour later, taken her to his apartment, she had felt herself in the grip of an irresistible force. And once she had become his, she loved him with an unassuming and unconditional ecstasy. The Slav blood, which among the men of her race erupted in hatred and revolt, had bred in her an emotional exuberance which now opened the floodgates. The shock of realisation that there was nothing she could do about it filled her with joy and dread.

The days that followed were filled with delight. She walked round the city with Severin, as he had been doing for years. She developed an ear for nuances of sound and distant cries such as he possessed and that he taught her. She closed her eyes and let him lead her, learning to recognise the street she was in by the smell the stones and asphalt gave off. And he opened her eyes to the monotonous beauty in the landscapes of the working-class districts, to the awesome majesty of the Vyšehrad with its massive stone portals and the memorial to St. Wenceslas. She came to love the Moldau, when the lights from the shore shimmered on the water in the darkness, and the smell of tar on the suspension bridges. She sat with him in the taverns of the Kleinseite, the quarter below the Hradschin, the castle hill on the left bank of the Moldau, entranced by the unhurried calm of the old burghers drinking their daily beer. The low vaulted ceilings were wreathed in thick cigar smoke, the pictures of Napoleon on the walls little more than smudges of grey. She went with him to the Vikárka on the Hradschin, where the cathedral with all the niches filled with statues and fantastic decoration on the walls towered up only a few arm's lengths from the door of the inn. She gradually came to understand the silent language of the city, with which Severin was more familiar than she was, even though she was Czech. She realised that he had grown up with a sense of the uncanny pervading its blackened walls, its towers and aristocratic town houses, its strange air of lifelessness, so that every time he went out into its streets it was with the feeling that some destiny awaited him.

When spring and summer came she was with him by the ponds of the Arboretum, feeding the swans. Or she took the ferry with him down the Moldau to Troja. Or they went through the gates of the ramparts and fortifications out to Pankrác and sat together at one of the stone tables in the inn garden where the one-eyed general of the Hussites, Jan Žižka, had rested during the Bohemian Wars. Not far away was the prison, like a miniature city in the middle of the fields, and on the lawns the convicts could be seen digging with their spades. Beyond the row of one-storey houses the road lead to the next village then away into the forest. The tune of a hurdy-gurdy mingled with the rustle of the poplars and the hum of the telegraph poles. Carriages with people out for the day passed, raising the thick layer of dust for the wind to blow to one side of the road. Sometimes they went to the 'Green Foxes', a roadside tavern. Years ago, when Severin was still a child, it had sold excellent beer and good food, and many Prague Germans used to make the carters' inn the destination of their Sunday walks. Now there was dancing every Sunday and the red-and-white Czech flags fluttered over the door. But a few steps further on there was a merry-go-round. Sometimes Zdenka would take a ride on it with Severin in one of the golden boats. A man in high boots beat the drum and the children screamed with delight. The music that played was the barcarole from *The Tales of Hoffmann*.

They were blissful hours for Zdenka. She scarcely noticed the times when Severin was taciturn or brusque; the next smile he gave her made up for it. But when autumn set in and Severin became more and more of a stranger, she felt a despondency she had never known before. Sometimes she would not see him for days on end. In mute sadness she made her way home and sat in her little room. All was movement in the square below her window, apart from the porters lounging at the corners. Zdenka waited until it was completely dark; she did not light the lamp until it was very late.

With a cruelty that was as pointless as it was incomprehensible, he had told her about Susanna. As he described his adventure in minute detail, his cold gaze scrutinised her face for a spark of jealousy. It annoyed him that her love remained steadfast and undiminished and that no reproach crossed her lips. It brought back to mind the girl in the play whose movements Zdenka had reminded him of. He remembered the way the slim, fragile figure had stood there on the stage while fate dealt her bitter blows. But all he saw as he looked at Zdenka was the shadow of a pain flit across her face, and even then he was not sure he had not been mistaken.

Their meetings on Sundays were growing less and less frequent. When they did meet they usually walked round the various gardens in the city where the cold autumn flowers were already in fiery bloom. Now and then they also took the funicular railway up Petřín Hill. Zdenka would stop to look at the pictures of the Stations of the Cross where the people went to pray every year on the eve of Good Friday. The Chapel of St Lawrence was also there. From the top they could see the city in the late afternoon haze as a lethargic breeze swept the dry leaves into the stone gutters beside the footpaths. With her foot Zdenka squashed the white berries that rolled onto the ground from the bushes. As a child she had always liked to hear the brief pop they made as they burst. A soldier coming along the path towards them bent down to his girl and kissed her. Zdenka walked beside Severin, her soul full of tears.

4

The guests were already gathered in Dr. Konrad's studio when Lazarus Kain and Severin arrived. They were greeted by a babble of voices that emerged from the cigarette smoke, an unusual mixture of conversations in German and in Czech, shot through with the brittle laughter of the women. At a table in one corner a number of strikingly dressed painters' models were amusing themselves with some Italian game of dice. Leaning casually against the door-jamb next to the blond Rušena was the marvellously slim figure of a lady in a black velvet dress who was observing the company. Severin recognised her at once. With the immediacy and sharpness of something that he had just seen, a long-forgotten image surfaced in his memory. As a boy in his final year at school he had once during the holidays been walking down Ferdinandstrasse at the time when the world of fashion paraded. She had stood out with the huge blood-red ostrich feather in her hat, her rare and elegant slenderness, her delightful and dangerous smile, a smile such as he had only seen on one other face, on a picture of the repentant Magdalene. A handsome young man had come up to her and greeted her, kissing the tips of her gloved fingers. It was a moment that had lodged in his memory and now came to life again: the holiday bustle in the street, the smooth sound of the rubber wheels of the carriages on the cobbles and, in the middle of the crush of people and splendid outfits, that one movement of ineffable grace with which the unknown woman had held out her hand for the young dandy to kiss. He had seen her several times after that, brief, unobserved encounters, then he had not seen her for a long time. She was a singer at the Czech National Theatre who had been at the height of her popularity when he first saw her. Kain, who had observed his fixed stare, told him her story. An illness she caught from one of her lovers had led to the loss of her voice. She had done the rounds of the provincial theatres until her voice gave up completely. Now she was back in Prague and Kain had already seen her several times in Dr. Konrad's studio.

It was not the custom in these circles for the guests to be introduced to each other. Everyone came and went as they pleased. Despite that, when their host greeted the new arrivals Severin asked him to introduce him to the lady in black. He stood and bowed as Dr. Konrad told her his name. He scrutinised her face for a sign of the grace of that one moment. Then he took the hand she held out to him and kissed it. She gave him a look of astonishment and smiled, but it was not the smile he remembered. Her lips were white and without make-up and fixed in a suggestion of affected indifference.

'Where is your hat with the red ostrich feather?' Severin asked.

'Oh', she exclaimed in surprise. She raised her head and swivelled it back and forward, as if she were remembering a dream. Then she said, slowly and in a dry, slightly husky voice, 'My hat with the red feather? That went a long time ago . . .'

Severin spent the whole evening at Karla's side. The party had gradually become louder and Rušena, the blonde done up like a doll, fetched her mandoline. The model girls had given up playing dice and were sitting at the table, gossiping, eating sandwiches and tossing back the champagne the servant was handing round. Lazarus Kain had joined them and was recounting his anecdotes. Some of the men had come with their girls and they were now sitting in the comfortable studio chairs, chewing and showing off their legs under their short skirts. Sitting beside Dr. Konrad was an incredibly skinny man in a fashionable frock coat and with an aristocratic manner. Various guests held out their hands to him and he read the future from the lines in their palms. Severin also went over and asked to have his fortune told. The skinny person gave him a searching look through his round spectacles and held Severin's hand in front of his face longer than the others.

'Fate has dealt you a blow', he said, when he looked up again, 'a harsh blow. What was it?'

'Nothing has happened to me', said Severin, withdrawing his hand.

'Then it is to come. You have a hand to put fear in a man's heart.'

Severin went back and sat down beside Karla again. He was annoyed with himself for having accepted the invitation and coming up to the studio with the bookseller, who was sitting contentedly among the tarts enjoying himself, his angular shoulders jerking up and down and his bald scalp quivering. Severin listened to the din with a feeling of sadness and disgust. Broad swathes of tobacco smoke rose and wreathed themselves round the light from the lamp which was suspended from the ceiling on elaborately wrought chains. From time to time Dr. Konrad went from one group to another, playing the host with the exaggerated politeness of the Slav. He was a tall man with a full beard, probably about thirty years old. With his dinner jacket he was wearing an ornate, light-coloured waistcoat with blue buttons. There was a dash of the Tartar about his intelligent, handsome face. Severin watched him and tried to fathom what it could be that made this man, whose doctorate sounded so out of place in his chosen environment, spend his days in extravagant and empty debauchery. Severin found nothing erotic about a gathering where, with brazen elegance, a few models pulled their skirts up above their knees, and that pretty doll Rušena twanged her mandoline and sang sentimental ballads and obscene songs, where the women got drunk on champagne and old Lazarus brought out his whole repertoire of puns. More than ever he thirsted for real life, for the life that brought flowers and horrors and storm winds that blew away the banalities of the mundane world. Until now he had had to make do with surrogates: his affair with Zdenka, so completely the opposite of a grand passion, his little adventure with Susanna, and now this bleak orgy in Konrad's studio where he was sitting morosely at Karla's side. He gave the slim singer a sidelong glance, studying the lines a life of changing fortunes had etched on the fine skin of her face. He knew that very shortly she too would be his. He radiated a force that drew women irresistibly to him, that filled them with the urge to kiss his tight, taciturn lips. Here, too, he could see them all smiling at him with their veiled eyes, even the blond Rušena was sending him fiery glances. And on the upholstered arm of the chair beside him lay Karla's slender hand which the handsome young man had kissed all those years ago. She knew the theatre and she knew life. He wanted to ask her if it would be possible to create an artificial life for oneself that would be a mirror image of the real one, but that one could control at will. Would it not be possible to incorporate tragedies into one's daily existence, operettas with deep messages that reverberated in one's mind for days afterwards? The stage was only play-acting and yet the people wept and cheered. Crimes were committed and fear beat its wings against the paper walls. Was it so difficult to create a destiny for oneself and others out of the heart's whims and quirks, just as they made landscapes and cities out of wood and cardboard in the theatre?

Karla just slowly shook her head.

'But why? Why?'

'Things just happen. That's the way it is.'

'No! No!' cried Severin. 'That's not true!'

Severin's cry throbbed with measureless protest, with an incandescent yearning such as many of those in the room felt and which rebounded like an echo from the smoke-grimed walls of the studio. There was a sudden silence as the conversations stopped and everyone turned towards Severin. Rušena put down her mandoline, her eyes fixed on his passion-filled face. Karla's fingers plucked nervously at her dress as she bent down towards him. The fervent beauty of former days struggled to reassert itself in the tattered remains of her husky voice, producing a sound like the tone of a cracked glass. She told him of the splendour of the life she had led when she still wore the hat with the red ostrich feather, of the youth whom Severin had seen in the street and who had loved her. She spoke of the sloughs and morasses of fortune. She whispered and halted, and suddenly the delightful Magdalene smile, that he had been looking for in vain all evening, was back on her lips.

Severin was seized with a feverish determination to enjoy himself. He raised his glass to Karla and emptied it. He poured glass after glass of the cool, sparkling wine down his throat until the studio blurred into a chaos of figures and faces as Rušena, skirts and frizzy hairpiece flying, began to dance a cancan on the rug in the centre of the room.

5

Since the party, a kind of friendship had grown up between Severin and Nikolaus, the man who had amused Dr. Konrad's guests with his palmistry. There was something indefinite and unfathomable about young student that attracted Severin and made him seek out his company. No one knew anything about Nikolaus, who had come to Prague a few years ago to read philosophy at the university. He could be seen playing football and tennis at the Belvedere sports grounds, he could be met in the boat-houses and rowing clubs by the Moldau. The evenings he spent sitting in the city's coffee houses, playing chess with all kinds of people for hours on end and drinking countless glasses of arrack punch through a narrow straw. It was known that he was rich, possessed a large and valuable library, sought the company of artists and interested himself in the occult. His elegantly and tastefully decorated apartment was full of strange and unusual objects, bronze cross-legged Buddhas, drawings done in a state of trance hanging on the walls in metal frames, scarabs and magic mirrors, a portrait of Madame Blavatsky and a genuine confessional. There was a story that once someone had died in his room under mysterious circumstances. There had been no witnesses, and the investigating magistrate came to the conclusion that a revolver, a particularly fine and valuable item, which Nikolaus had been showing to his visitor, had suddenly gone off without warning and killed him. The proceedings against Nikolaus were abandoned, but a persistent rumour linked a society lady with the accident. There was talk of manslaughter, or a duel by drawing lots, and Nikolaus did not seem to feel the need to deny the stories.

The story of the mysterious death of the young man made an enormous impression on Severin. Now he started spending the occasional evening in his new acquaintance's apartment, sipping the thick liqueurs his host served in matt coloured glasses and gazing at his gaunt features with unconcealed awe. His eyes kept being drawn to the delicate lady's writing-desk where sharp-edged knives lay among a scatter of books and papers and where, he suspected, behind the yellow brass locks lay the pistol which had called up Death in this room. Death. There was something in the dull sound of that one syllable that seemed to him more stimulating, more suggestive than all the drowsy expressions of a sheltered life. Tiny, warped bubbles of envy floated up from the depths of his soul, forming a scum on the surface that was slow to disperse. It was envy of Nikolaus, who could play nonchalantly with the opal ring on his finger and chat about books and magazines while the carpet under his feet still perhaps held traces of the blood of the man who had died on it. He felt the superiority of a man who could hide his true nature from the world behind a blasé correctness of behaviour, whose character, despite his youth, had nothing of the tentativeness and lack of definition of his own.

Karla, too, sometimes came with him to visit Nikolaus in his room. Since she had met Severin she followed him wherever he went and managed to arrange things so that she ran into him almost daily. For her deep-feeling soul, that had been through ice and fire, he was a new, as yet untasted fever and she had fallen completely under his spell. She pursued him with the obstinate determination of a young girl in love, the unaffected yearning of her melancholy nature, and all the artfulness of an experienced and ruthless cocotte. Severin found himself unable to resist the power of her personality, but his experience with Karla followed the same pattern as all others so far. There were moments when his heart seemed to be on the threshold of something for which he had no name but towards which he felt he was groping his way through the dark. At such moments their hands slipped, trembling, into each other. Everything around him was bathed in a special, golden radiance as he sat silent and still, open to the spellbinding beauty of the things of the world around him. Then there were other times when the glory departed entirely. He felt sad and angry that he had allowed a momentary mood to deceive him. He saw the glint in Karla's eyes, her tall, slim body, her free-and-easy posture. He saw the pale, uncertain shadows of the promiscuous dusk descending on an earth suddenly bereft of wonder. And he kissed Karla on the lips and took her, just as he had taken Susanna and would take Rušena if she should ask him.

He talked with Nikolaus about his feelings. He told him of all the thoughts that went through his mind as he wrote out the columns of figures on grey paper during the mornings with the light of the bare bulb flickering on the wet ink. He talked about the book he had read as a boy, about the fear that sometimes seized him as he stood at the door of his apartment, unable for minutes on end to find the courage to open it, as if the very act of unlocking it would bring about something momentous and decisive. He told him about his love affairs, as far as he could remember all the experiences of nights of drunken revelry in low bars and music halls. He always believed he had been touched in his innermost heart, had sensed within himself a movement beyond the power of the will, that came and went of its own accord, that overpowered all the others, that drove women to throw themselves into the Moldau and men to press the barrel of a revolver to their temples. Once he had been present when some raftsmen had pulled the corpse of a woman out of the water on the embankment at Podskal. It had been a young working-class woman, a servant or artisan's wife, and her wet clothes had stuck to her rigid body, clinging to her powerful thighs and round breasts. Severin arrived as people were gathering round the corpse and the policeman was making notes. He looked at her blue lips, her features, twisted in their death-throes, and wondered what kind of life such a person must have led, what violence or distress could have brought it to such an end. Every day he read reports of suicides in the newspapers. Now it was two people who had shot themselves in a hotel room, now a girl who had taken poison and died in an agony of pain. Fifteen-year-old schoolboys, still scarcely more than children, killed themselves because they could not endure life any longer. Severin could not understand it. Defiant and alone, he observed the long procession of unfortunates who had been destroyed by love or hatred, he read in the newspaper court reports of those weary souls who hovered in despair, caught between contending fates. In his mind's eye he saw the growing number of victims and victors in this struggle and he knew that among those passing him in the street were people with burning souls, gamblers who would risk all on the turn of a card and bankrupts who were beyond even that.

Nikolaus listened to him, deep in thought, all the time pushing back the cuticle from his polished fingernails with a little ivory spatula. And when Severin told him of Zdenka and Susanna and the other the women he had known, and how in the arms of the barmaids, in the bed of the Jewish girl, in Karla's embrace he had looked in vain for the intoxication he hoped to feel coursing through his veins, he said, 'Women are nothing to you. I believe something greater lies in store for you.'

It shook Severin. He remembered the strange prophecy Nikolaus had read in the lines of his palm when they first met in Dr. Konrad's studio. He could feel the throb of his pulse, and with a tingle that set his hair on end he sensed the approach of some as yet obscure, unknown destiny, which he yearned for with every fibre in his body.

6

Winter arrived, suddenly and unexpectedly. When Severin came out of the house one morning the snow was lying on the roofs and pavements, swirling through the last scraps of darkness over the city. It was eight o'clock and the shops in the street were opening their shutters with a laborious clattering. The wind brought a chill to the snow-covered streets and Severin felt slightly cold in his thin overcoat. He was surprised and walked slowly to the office, taking a short detour. For the first time in years he was conscious of the fact that snow had a smell of its own, like apples that had been kept for a long time between the panes of the double windows. Even as a child he had been sensitive to the aroma clinging to each and every thing and time. He thought back to those first days of a new school term and the damp smell of chalk that greeted him as he entered the classroom again. He recalled the feeling of well-being on the morning when, after a long and heavy frost, he could feel the thaw through the cracks in the door and then, outside, sipped the meltwater that trickled down in glittering threads from the trees and window-ledges and tasted quite different, milder, in the sun than in the shade. His childhood had been filled with this delight in all kinds of smells, smells which gladdened or oppressed him, which betokened continuity and return, and which accompanied the seasons. Now he was glad that autumn was over and winter had come. He felt as if something new had happened, something for which he had been looking for a long time.

In the office he sat still, keeping his head below the high shelves and drawers at the front of his desk and looking out through the dirty windows at the white stars drifting down into the courtyard. On his way there he had walked past stalls selling things for St. Nicholas. The carved wooden devils were sticking their red flannel tongues out at him and at the street corners there were whole thickets of golden sticks for his servant to threaten naughty children with. Rows of St Nicholases in stiff clothes and with a cotton-wool beard stood on green shelves.

In the evening he went to the advent fair in the Old Town Square. People were crowding between stalls with gingerbread soldiers, yellow trumpets and brightly coloured toy drums, and girls pushed their way through the throng in pairs. The storm lanterns swayed over the display of candy, flickering on the red turbans of the men selling Turkish delight. Beside the low tent of a waxworks show he caught sight of Zdenka leaning against a post, staring at the negro sitting at the desk selling tickets. It was a long time since Severin had last seen her. When he suddenly touched her arm she she gave a startled cry.

'You – you –', she stammered and her beautiful voice cracked, giving way under the strain of tears. But then she took his hands and led him to a quiet alley away from the bustle of the market. By the light of a street lamp she looked at his face. And he saw how drawn and wretched her's had become. Her nose was gaunt and pointed, like a sick person's, and her lips were thin. All that was left was the sweetness in the careworn corners and shadows round her eyes, which she fixed on him with a look that he had not seen before in her. She wanted to speak, but could not. And seeing her standing there before him, helpless and confused, overcome with love, Severin felt within himself, besides pity for Zdenka, the stirrings of a self-satisfied pleasure in her pain. He compared her with his memory of the girl in the play that he could not get out of his mind whenever he was with Zdenka. He thought to himself that now the play was over and it was time for the curtain to fall. In the gesture with which he stroked her cheek and brushed back the hair that was falling in her face there was something of his old tenderness of the summer that was past. With an anguished cry she fell at his feet and clasped his knees with her hands.

'Severin –'

Some people on their way home from the fair stopped a little way off and looked at the weeping girl crouched on the ground. Severin prised her hands from his knees and walked away without looking round.

In young Nikolaus' room there was a small cupboard decorated with precious stones and marquetry. When one day Severin asked him what it contained he took a slim key out of his pocket and opened it. Inside, carefully packaged and arranged in neat rows one above the other, were round red pellets of opium, poisonous powders in tiny glass tubes and Indian temple hashish in flat chemist's pillboxes.

'I'm a collector', said Nikolaus.

Tingling with excitement, Severin stood for a long time spellbound looking at the open cupboard. His eyes roamed round the inside, probing every one of the elegant compartments where the secrets of foreign cultures were stored, substances that brought dreams and visions, filling the blood with an intoxication of lasciviousness, poisons that could kill. They gave off a fragrance that caressed the senses. With a smile, Nikolaus observed the tautness of excitement in his face and took a blue phial with a glass stopper out of one corner of the cupboard.

'This one's guaranteed', he said, 'but you must be careful.'

'What is it?'

'A Chinese poison.'

'And you're giving it to me?'

Nikolaus slowly pushed the door of the cupboard to. 'I've plenty of the stuff.' And he turned the key in the lock.

As Severin was going down the stairs he ran into Karla. For days now she had been hoping he would come and was on her way to Nikolaus' apartment, where she assumed she would find him. Her black velvet dress was trailing over the steps and for a few moments she drew herself up and turned towards him. Her face was white, as if she had come to some decision.

'Where are you?'

Severin raised his eyes to hers, which were moving over his body, absent, dark. In them he could see her fear of losing him. He examined her tall, regal figure, stretching up towards him from the stone stairs like an exotic, yearning flower, and saw that in that moment she was beautiful. He imagined he could see on her lips the marks of the kisses he had drunk only a short while ago. But it was like something long past, something that he had long put behind him which could not touch his soul any more. With a great effort, like someone in their sleep seeking words they cannot remember, he said, 'Go home Karla. I do not love you any longer.'

Her hand slipped from the edge of the banister. A gust of wind came through the open house door, making them both shiver.

'Go home', he said again and walked past her, just as he had left Zdenka, without turning his head.

In his room Severin stood in the darkness for a while. He felt in his pocket for the phial. It had absorbed the warmth from his body, and he realised how cold his hands were. He lit the candle.

On the table was a letter, his name on the envelope written in a woman's sloping, lascivious hand. A messenger must have brought it while he was at Nikolaus'. He opened it and looked for the signature. Without reading it, he held the blond-haired Rušena's letter over the candle flame.

7

Since Severin had had the powder from his friend's poison cabinet in his possession he found he was in the grip of an irresistible restlessness. He was completely alone again and avoided all company. He no longer went to see Nikolaus and it was weeks now since he had been to visit old Lazarus. The last time had been on the day when he had met him in the street and gone with him to Dr Konrad's studio. He had not heard anything at all from Susanna. Since that autumn evening when, in a sudden blaze of passion, she had taken him to her room, he had had no news from her. He deliberately kept away from her father's shop, following his predilection for unclear, indeterminate situations. He was afraid the usual sequel would trivialise his memory of the Jewess, rob it of its magic. He was prey to all the vague desires of a person who managed to observe his own experiences even while in the middle of them. It suited him that Susanna made no attempt to see him, and he had finished with Karla and Zdenka. There was a constant quiver of longing gnawing at his bemused heart. Once again he had started lying down when he came home from work in the afternoons and sinking into a dull sleep that could last for hours. Then at night he would lie awake in his bed, staring into the darkness. He counted the hours as he heard them struck by the clock in the neighbouring apartment and fought against the fear that assailed him. In the morning he went to the office with red-rimmed eyes.

It sometimes happened that he woke in the middle of the night with the urge to get dressed. He could no longer bear to be in the tangled sheets of his bed, in the long, low room which the darkness seemed unwilling to leave; it was still dark there, even though outside the sky was streaked with the first dim light of dawn. He often found himself, two or three hours after midnight, locking the door of his apartment behind him and feeling his way down the pitch-black stairs to the street. The city, which he was used to wandering round by day or in the evening, had acquired an unknown, covert power over him. It was dragging him out of his timid dreams into its dark womb. Shivering, a burnt-out cigarette between his lips, he would walk past the sleeping houses, peering into the late-night light of lonely windows, listening to the singing of revellers on their way home or to the heavy tread of the policemen. There had been a time when he too, eyes still hot from the wine and wearied by the din in the taverns, had often made his way home late at night. Only now did he notice the difference. His senses were alert and wide awake. He saw how all things were changed by night, how they lived a second, different life from their daytime existence. He saw how it transformed bare, ordinary squares into melancholy land-scapes, narrow streets into damp-walled castle dungeons. His restlessness drove him to the farthest corners of the working-class districts with their endless rows of tenements, to the fifth district with its monotonous modern streets where one could get lost even by day. Here and there a few remnants of the old Jewish quarter crept out of the darkness, the Monastery of the Hospitallers thrust its immense torso out against the encroaching modern buildings still swathed in scaffolding. On the Francis Embankment there were just a few isolated lamps burning and the waters of the river slapped against the bridge in a heavy, regular rhythm.

In the late-night taverns the musicians were playing their hoarse violins. Severin stood at the murky window-panes, peering in through the curtains. He heard the clack of the billiard balls on the green baize and the clatter of crockery from the buffet. When the door opened the insipid smell of early-morning soup wafted out into the street. The winter was cold and Severin dug his hands with their aching joints deep into his pockets. Now and then he went in to listen to the music. Then he would order a bowl of flaming punch and warm his fingers over the blue flames. The stale cigarette smoke made his eyes smart but the warmth was comforting.

It was usually the same taverns where Severin hid from the cold: the 'White Garland' at the fruit market, where the customers simply pillowed their heads on their arms and went to sleep, sprawled over the table; the 'Crease' in Little Charles Street, where for hours he was often the only customer; or the Russian coffee house somewhere on the fringe between Prague and Vinohrady, which was frequented by the Serbian, Bosnian and Slovenian students. He knew all these places from the time when he spent his nights in pursuit of amorous adventure. Now he sat there without expectation, without a sense of belonging, in a world that seemed unreal, a world of automatons, in low dives where a last residue of revelry sank beneath the weight of its own grossness, and in coffee houses where the benches were upholstered in red velvet and waiters as well as guests looked like roués. He had to laugh at himself when he remembered how he had hoped these would be the places where he would quench the thirst that tormented his soul. Years had passed since then and there had been no inner transformation. He had become more bitter, obstinate and self-willed, that was all. The agitation that beset him was the feverishness that comes from lack of sleep and had nothing to do with the ferment of debauchery around him, and the torpor that paralysed him was different from that on the faces of the whores lolling at their tables, who sometimes came over to him to beg a glass of tea. He no longer knew how many days or weeks now he had been wandering round the city at night, hanging out in the taverns that stayed open until morning. But he felt he was going in a circle round the same point, like an animal tethered on a chain. Almost faint with horror, he patted his clothes for the phial of poison he kept in one of his pockets. After one of these sleepless night, as the winter morning was creeping along the streets, he made his way to Nikolaus' apartment.

It was still early when, with a hasty, sullen ring, the bell sounded in the vestibule. Nikolaus was still in bed and greeted his visitor with undisguised astonishment. But when he saw Severin's face, wasted and hollow-eyed, he held out his hand to him.

Nikolaus' bedroom resembled a boudoir. His refined taste had brought together a hundred artistic objects which turned the room into something more like a courtesan's sumptuous nest than a bachelor's bedroom. From the ceiling hung a silver lamp with honey-coloured glass, bathing the room in a warm light. The chairs and small tables glowed with the rich colours of silks and brocades. There were dark bronze statuettes, sandalwood boxes and Japanese painted lacquerwork beside delicate glasses and caskets, communion chalices and Asiatic ornaments. A huge candelabrum, black with age, held seven thick ceremonial candles in its arms. The first, dreary glimmers of a winter's day were filtering in through the Gothic design on the curtain. Severin's eyes went round the room, over the matt lines of the wallpaper to the place where Nikolaus was sitting, half propped up, in his golden bed. They had an expression as if they were disoriented by the surroundings, by the tasteful opulence of the décor. As he grasped the hand Nikolaus held out to him, he let out a cry which gave vent to all his torment and distress. He knelt beside the young man's bed and burrowed his head into the pillows.

'Nikolaus', he cried, 'what was it like . . . when you killed your friend?'

Nikolaus looked down at Severin. His body was stretched out on the floor in unspeakable convulsions, fear suffused his face with blood and he raised his arm, holding it in the air with the fingers splayed. There was a deep, pitying sadness in his voice as he repeated the other man's name, 'Severin! Severin!'

8

Doctor Konrad was dead. After a night of riotous noise in which the company had gathered in his apartment for the last time, he had put a bullet through his head. Death had come to him with the same inchoate futility that had characterised his life. His body lay on the floor beside the Turkish sofa, among broken glasses and cigarette ends still soggy from spilt wine. Blood ran out of the small wound in his temple onto the parquet floor. In that last night he had spent all that remained of his fortune. After the guests had left he shot himself.

It was a motley group of mourners that accompanied his coffin: young graduates in threadbare overcoats, their frost-reddened hands thrust deep in their pockets and their faces, as they gazed on the coffin, full of sincere mourning: the man they were accompanying to his last rest had always been generous to them; wastrels with bohemian hats and debauched faces; demi-mondaines in tightly fitting dresses which showed their legs as they walked; elegant women in furs and huge muffs, and gentlemen in carefully brushed top hats preening themselves seductively in their fashionably waisted winter overcoats. Rušena, Konrad's blond-haired mistress, walked behind the hearse. Severin had gone up to her and silently given her his hand. She responded with an angry glint in her eyes, but she said nothing. Her expressionless face, which had a little too much make-up, gave no hint that she had meant more to the dead man that all the rest. Severin gave her a piercing look, but she looked away.

Karla was walking beside a large, thin-lipped man. Her tall figure seemed if possible even slimmer than before and she stooped slightly. Her wide coat hung loose about her and she walked with uncertain, shuffling steps completely lacking the arrogant grace Severin associated with her. In the few weeks since he had met her on the stairs her face had aged and withered and he found it impossible to tell whether the colour in her cheeks came from cosmetics or the cold. The procession came to a halt outside the National Museum at the top of Wenceslas Square. The priest blessed the coffin and the crowd of mourners dispersed. Only his closest acquaintances followed the coffin to the cemetery in cabs.

Severin went too. With his handkerchief he wiped the windows clear of the condensation which was slowly turning to ice round the edges of the panes. Outside, the dreary and monotonous panorama of Wolschaner Strasse was rolling by. He had not attended a funeral since he was a child. He remembered how the cab he had been in with his parents had got mixed up with a demonstration of Czech nationalists returning home after the funeral of one of their martyrs in the graveyard. A battle-hymn sung by a thousand voices came pouring menacingly down the street towards them, causing the horses to rear then stand still, quivering. Severin, listening to the rumbling of the wheels, remembered the exquisite sensation of fear mingled with awe and dread that had gripped him.

It was already almost dark when he got out of the cab at the cemetery outside the town. He stood beside Karla as the frozen earth tumbled into the grave, clattering on the coffin-lid. Only now that he was close to her could he see how yellow and withered her face looked. The powder lay on her cheeks in round flakes and her beautiful voice was thin and sad. Standing beside the open grave here in the cemetery he saw how it was her destiny to pass from one heartache to the next, from one lover to the next. She gave a start when, with a questioning glance, he indicated the large man with whom she had come. Softly, gently, as if speaking to a child, he asked, 'And he's . . .?'

'Yes', she replied with a nod.

Severin made his way back to the city on foot. He paid off the cabbie and was the last to leave the cemetery after the others had already gone. The fields were swathed in the pale violet of the late afternoon and from far off came the muffled rumble of a railway train. Here and there beside the road stood a tree stretching its bare branches out against the gloomy sky. As the evening filled the fields it cast straggling shadows among the turnips. Mist was rising and in the twilight the sparrows flying across the road were like huge black birds. The electric tram drove past with its yellow eyes, and the lights went on in the city. Severin was thinking about Konrad's death. A flaccid, grotesque fancy had planted itself in Severin's brain and refused to leave. He kept seeing the face of the man they had just buried as it lay in the earth, under the coffin lid. A chill crept over his skin, making him shiver, like the clouds on the horizon. He felt his pulse, but he was not at all afraid. In the distance there were white figures writhing and turning, but he knew it was only the winter mist. The first houses of Vinohrady loomed up out of the greyness. He looked back the way he had come. The air hung slack and motionless in the sky and the frost had intensified. The light from the shop windows was already falling on the pavements of the outer suburbs.

Severin stopped by the door of a horse-butcher's. He was immediately enveloped in a warm smell of blood, and nausea gripped him. Two men in rolled-up shirt sleeves carried out a steaming bowl which mingled with the cold in a vile stench. With fastidious care Severin buttoned up his gloves before he touched the grubby doorknob. A broad-shouldered man with red hair gave him a suspicious look when he asked for a few coppers' worth of meat. He left the shop carrying a soft, sticky package wrapped in newspaper. By the light of a street lamp he cautiously undid the string and opened it. He took the phial of poison out of his pocket and poured the contents over the meat. He looked closely at the fine dry powder gleaming among the bloody fibres.

Susanna was sitting by the stove listening to the fire when Severin entered. She was holding her hand over her eyes as if she were asleep and peeped through her fingers at the door. Old Lazarus had gone out and the chair behind his desk was empty.

'Good evening, Susanna', said Severin.

Susanna raised her head in a slow spurt of astonishment.

Her shoulders quivered and the furrow between her brows deepened and darkened as she returned his greeting. Then, with a strange note in her voice, she asked him, 'Where have you come from, Severin?'

Severin did not answer. He stood there, irresolute. He could feel a sensation which he knew well but had not experienced for a long time gradually seeping through his body. When he had been a student it had sometimes come over him as he sat at home reading old English novels while the lamp beside him hummed. It seemed as if the room were becoming part of the story in which he was immersed. Silhouettes of the characters whose destinies he was following would start to flit across the wall opposite and in the dim light filling the room he recognised their gestures.

Finally he spoke. 'Doctor Konrad is dead', he said, sitting down beside the desk in the chair with the leather-upholstered arms. He looked past Susanna at the picture hanging in the corner behind her that he had never noticed before. It was a landscape with a bizarre and dreamlike tree beneath which a number of people were walking in the semi-dark. He felt a current of air waft across his cheek; the raven had abandoned its perch behind him and flew down onto his knee. Severin bent over the bird. Slowly he took the poisoned meat out of his pocket.

'This is death', he said, holding it under its beak. The bird snatched it from him and flew back up to its perch with it.

Severin looked across at Susanna. Her heavy braids had come loose and slipped down into her lap. Her expression was cold and inscrutable, and her lips were pressed tightly together. It was perfectly quiet in the shop, the footsteps of the people passing along the pavement outside could be heard. Reflections flickered across the surface of the glowing stove, projecting figures onto the canvas.

Severin was searching through his memory. The tree on the picture looked familiar to him, he had seen it somewhere before, but could not remember where.

I'm leaving, he thought and stood up.

'Goodbye, Susanna', he said, taking his hat. Then he cocked an ear towards the corner where the raven had withdrawn with its food. There was no sign of movement.

9

The storm had come during the night and was coursing up and down the streets, bellowing furiously. From the plain beyond the mountains where the border ran it had brought a heavy, steamy warmth with it and was splashing the meltwater off the roofs. Severin lay awake in the darkness. Fever was drenching his body in sweat and setting his blood on fire. The window rattled, and every now and then there came a dull groan from below as the door of the house writhed on its hinges. For a moment the room was lit by the yellow flash of a winter thunderstorm and suddenly Severin thought he could see in its light the picture hanging above Susanna's head in the bookshop. Now he remembered where he had seen the tree before. It was at Konrad's funeral, by the wall in the part of the cemetery set aside for new graves. Severin had kept his eyes fixed on it while they were lowering the coffin into the earth and it had appeared strange and grotesque to him.

He pulled the cover up to his neck. He was shivering. Without being able to account for it, he felt a great sorrow oppressing him. He thought of the foolish, cruel visit he had made the previous day, of how he had killed the raven. Outside, the storm shattered the glass rattling in the street lamps and flew gurgling down the chimney.

He was weary from lack of sleep as he made his way to the office in the morning. In the streets the water spread out in broad puddles and the wind was still blowing violently. His hat flew off his head and landed in the mud. Severin bent down and put it back on. A chilly trickle of slime ran down over his forehead from the brim, but he ignored it. During the morning, while he was writing and adding up columns of figures, an occasional flurry of rain kept drumming on the window-panes. Severin stood up and looked out at the wet cobbles down in the courtyard. He felt a faint nausea sliding up his throat like a smooth ball. He went home earlier than usual and tumbled back into bed, but sleep would not come.

Whenever he closed his eyes he had the sensation of falling, constantly, unstoppably. And all the time there was an obscure idea lodged in his temples like a burning ember. Struck with horror, he buried his face in the pillow.

The wind had subsided and it had turned almost sultry. In the city night was already falling and all that was left of the day were the blue-black outlines the departing light drew round the clouds over the houses. Head bent, Severin walked among the people. An immense fear hung from his heart like a weight, making him stumble. A heavy object in his pocket was pressing against him and he curled his fingers round it. It was a large round stone he had once picked up in the fields and taken home.

The gaslight was burning over the desk in Lazarus Kain's bookshop. Through the glass door Severin could see the bookseller's bald, pointed head. There was a furrow running down the middle towards the forehead, as if the skin were stretched over a split bone. Severin shivered. He looked to the back of the shop for the picture and a tortured smile froze on his lips as he recognised the tree he had dreamed of during the night.

A hand was placed on his shoulder. He turned round and saw Susanna standing before him.

'What are you doing here?' she asked, and he could feel the menace in her expressionless eyes. In the twilight her figure grew tall and imperious. Horrified, Severin saw that she was expecting a child.

'Susanna!' he whispered.

For the first time in weeks a light penetrated his naked soul. To his consternation, the darkness within him began to disperse.

Why have I come here? he asked himself. The bleak alley was quiet and unfrequented and the face of the Jewish girl filled him with fear. The hand clutching the stone began to tremble and his heart stood still.

'But I'm not a murderer', he said out loud, and at the same moment he saw himself in an invisible mirror, disfigured by vices which were choking him, covered with sores festering with doom.

'Jesus!' he cried out, and it was his own voice which told him that he had come to murder Lazarus Kain.

'Jesus!'

His scream was so terrible that Susanna went pale. She felt her senses darken as unconsciousness crept over her and it was only hazily and with a fluttering heart that she saw Severin run down the lane into the darkness.

It was already late and the moon was standing, white and calm, above the towers. The clouds had dispersed and it had turned clear and colder. Severin walked along under the trees by the Belvedere in the Royal Gardens, breathing in the damp air, which already bore a taste of the coming spring. In the valley below lay the city. Here and there a few lights were still burning, like the eyes of some far-off, sleepy beast. A shiver ran down Severin's spine. He thought of the thousands down there who, like himself, were floundering in the morass of a dreary existence. He was overcome with the memory of the people he had encountered and who were doomed, each and every one of them. Karla who in desperation abandoned herself to insidious agonies, Konrad on whose grave the earth was still fresh, and Susanna who would give birth to his child while hating the father. He was oppressed by a sadness beyond bearing. He peered down into the shadows of the houses and saw a figure that was himself, wrapped up in the mysteries of love and death, restlessly roaming the streets and alleys where thoughts of murder seeped up out of the cobbles, casting a shadow over his heart. He wept, and his tears were as sharp and biting as vinegar. He hit his head against a tree-trunk until his forehead was bleeding, and sank his teeth into the bark. He was racked with a sense of desolation and longed for a face against which he could rest his own.

Suddenly he felt as if, out of the darkness, two eyes were fixed on him, eyes that he had long forgotten. A beautiful, friendly voice awoke in his memory and comforted him. He turned round and set off down towards the bridge.

The window of the little room on the Old Town Square was still lit. It was always the last one in the large building to go dark, a long time after the others. While sleep crouched on the thresholds and the bats flew in and out past the bells of the town hall clock, Zdenka was still awake and only went to bed when she was exhausted by the thoughts running through her mind and the lamp was beginning to flicker.

Severin had climbed the stairs and was waiting by the door. He knocked. He would have called out, but his voice refused to obey.

'Severin!'

She had pulled back the bolt and was standing in the light, flushed and dazed. Her blond hair was loose and fell down onto her dress; she was holding her hands against her breast. Her slim face was charming as she held up her lips to be kissed.

'I knew you would come back. I've been waiting for you . . .'

He knelt down before her and caressed her hands. He felt like a child that has been lost and has finally found its way home.

'I love you', he said and felt that at last it was true. Then he called out her name, tenderly, solemnly, as never before.

'Zdenka! Zdenka!'

Hand in hand they went over to the window and looked out into the night. From the streets came the raucous singing of the drunks. The moonlight was glistening on the window-panes. It hung like a flame over the roofs of the city, enveloping them in a white, smoky cloud. Severin felt that something miraculous was happening, something that was sweeter and more tremendous by far than the adventures in the book about the Thirty Years War. He bent down towards Zdenka, searching for her lips, and as he kissed her a booming noise came through the moonlight into the room, a growling crash, as if the earth had split.

In the Moldau the ice had started to break up.

Book Two
The Spider

1

Summer had slowly returned. Imperceptibly, one week after another had slipped past Severin's life without shaking his heart out of the exhaustion in which it had lain since the end of the winter. On that evening when he had shed tears of despair in Zdenka's room in the Old Town Square, he had not believed there was such a thing as peace. And now there was a wondrous tranquillity inside him, sharpening his senses, enfolding him as he smiled at the world like someone who has recovered from a serious illness. A tender alertness awoke within him through which he observed the thousand tiny details of life, like a foreigner to whom everything is new and who is forever astonished. Every day the dawn woke him from a long and even sleep, and the sun had risen outside his window, hot and shining, when he opened his eyes and then shut them, dazzled; or the warm rain, that he loved so well, pattered against the wall of his room, filling the air outside with sweet odours. He was together with Zdenka all the time now.

He felt afraid whenever a memory of the winter caught him unawares, and his love sought help from her. It was with a childlike reverence that he enjoyed her companionship, which, as in earlier days, led them on Sundays to various places of recreation in the city and suburbs. They sat together in beer-gardens, listening to concerts given by military bands, which would play a pot-pourri of pieces by Verdi and Wagner, popular tunes from Viennese operettas and the 'Reserve Officer's Dream'. The leaves of the chestnut trees spread like a green fanlight above them and cast bobbing patches of sunlight onto the table-cloths, to which dampness and the smell of clothes-pegs still clung. Severin fixed his gaze on Zdenka's beautiful face and placed his cigarette between his lips with the lethargy of a convalescent. He found the voices of the people chatting at the neighbouring tables soothing. In the scraps of conversation that reached him he could hear the well-ordered, cosily stifled rhythm of a life to which he abandoned himself contentedly.

That year, or so it seemed to him, the city had been more than usually transformed by the summer. His body still responded to the throb of its blood, but it no longer frightened him. In the afternoons, before he met Zdenka at the office where she worked, he would wander through the sunny streets. He would watch the men as they sprinkled the roads, delighting in the little fountains that spurted up from the damaged hosepipes and the colourful rainbows glinting through the fine spray. The acacias were in bloom along the embankment. Severin sat on a bench at the edge of the river bank. Below him flowed the Moldau and a sailing boat was slowly drifting down towards the mills. A swarm of fantastically shaped clouds crossed the sky, blotting out the sun for a while.

It was a scene Severin knew from his childhood. Then he had sometimes sat under the acacias on the embankment with his father, waiting for Aunt Regina. A musty memory raised its sleepy head in his mind and before his inner eye appeared the dark, ground-floor apartment, where his aunt had lived with an old lady. He had always liked going there to visit her. Behind the white tulle curtains had stood a weather-house with a little man carrying a red tin umbrella outside the door. The old lady was ill, cancer was eating up her frail body. She leased a small tobacco shop on Bethlehem Square, a wooden kiosk in the angle of the houses where she sat during the day selling cigars. In the sitting room, which she shared with Aunt Regina, there was always a strange mixture of smells, of fusty air from the cellar and withered Corpus Christi wreaths, of incense and the dry aroma of her stock of tobacco. For Severin it all had a special attraction, filled with a quiver of childish surmise. It was from his aunt's room, which was crowded with consecrated candles and pictures of saints, dog-eared hymn-books and crosses of coral, that his soul had taken home the first flickerings of the fervour which had haunted his childhood.

A little of this fervour stirred within Severin once more. He saw the Kleinseite on the other side of the river, and Charles Bridge with the priests of the religious orders in their long cassocks crossing it in pairs like school-children. There was something of the atmosphere of the feast of St. John Nepomuk left on the breeze, as it wafted calmly across the water and swept up the withered petals of the Moldau acacias at his feet. On the bridge the wooden trestle with the glass lamps was still standing before the statue of the martyr where each year the country people came from their villages to honour their patron saint. Severin remembered the fever of expectation that had accompanied the feast day of the Czech saint. On St. John's Eve he had gone with his father to the river bank where the flood of people had been piling up for hours. When darkness fell there had been a firework display and the thin rockets had shot straight up into the sky with a soft crackling noise. Down below, the boats floating on the river were hung with lights and the peasants on the bridge were praying before the statue of St. John Nepomuk.

Severin had not been inside a church for years. His youthful fire had been consumed in blind and casual enthusiasms. He was in the grip of a weariness which he allowed to carry him along aimlessly from one day to the next and from which the old, long-forgotten yearning of his boyhood soul now rose to the surface. From the scent of the acacias and the river air, the afternoon sun had brewed a warm haze with a hint of decay which excited him. An orphanage was taking a walk along the embankment path and the girls, all dressed the same, were whispering to each other. They were accompanied by a nun enveloped in her habit; for a brief second the young eyes beneath the cowl looked across at Severin. They were grey and pious eyes with a star glittering in the middle of the pupil, just as Aunt Regina's had been.

Uncertain what to do, he stood up and searched through his pockets for a cigarette. Opposite him the sign of the Bible Society was gleaming in the sun. Once, during the school holidays many years ago, he had bought a copy of the Scriptures there for a few coppers. He had not kept it for long; it had disappeared, as did most of the books he possessed. It only came back to mind because he felt a longing for the records of the Testaments, heavy and dark with age, and for the bright wisdom of the Evangelists.

Some children were playing in the sand by the monument to Emperor Francis. A white-bearded old man with a green eye-shade and a misshapen pair of spectacles was selling sticky sweets and *Brezels*, twisted bread sticks covered in salt crystals or poppy seeds. Severin bought the rest of his stock and shared it out amongst the children. The old man went off with an empty basket and a pleased look on his face; the servant girls on the benches nudged each other and giggled.

Severin was moved by a soft and blissful emotion which was interwoven with the long-faded objects of his school-days. His thoughts cautiously felt their way back into that world, to the naive magic of the school chapel, to his feeling of shyness whenever his fingertips touched the cool com-munion cloths. The music of the May services began to resound within him, when the organ united with the hymns to the Virgin and outside, where the lime tree grew beside the open church window, a bird warbled, loudly and with a throbbing throat.

He crossed the bridge, doffing his hat to the golden cruci-fix, and before he realised it, he was standing outside the portal of St. Nicholas' on the Kleinseite. Its green dome glittered above the roofs, and the sun fell on the steps up to the door with a burning, dazzling light. The stone faces of the bishops watched him out of the the richly hued gloom, and his steps echoed from the pillars. The church was empty apart from a woman in black kneeling not far from the door. When he entered she turned round, and he recognised the nun from the embankment. Her face was white and her eyes burnt beneath the cowl. Severin knelt next to her and said the 'Salve Regina' aloud. And he felt as if a startled smile crossed her lips behind her folded hands.

2

Together with her new friend, Karla had opened a wine tavern near the centre of the city. Close to the German University, with the students in their colourful caps standing beside the huge wooden doors, began a maze of winding alleys. Cool air came from the entries of the houses that stretched between the streets, and from the craftsmen's work-shops the smell of damp felt and mouldy leather. Sometimes pedlars who had brought mushrooms or fresh berries to the city would spend the night beside their baskets under the tree-lined arcades of the fruit and vegetable market. During the day there was a bustle of activity, people crowded the narrow pavements, junk dealers cried out their wares in lilting tones and carts rumbled over the bumpy cobbles. At night the noise went into hiding behind the murky windows of the little dance halls, except when a tipsy group passed by, or a policeman, surrounded by a circle of curious onlookers, dealt with a drunken brawl.

A fiery arc-lamp hung outside the tavern in the dark alley-way. Coming round the corner between the badly lit houses, the light was blinding and the muted sound of a piano came from the door. In decorating the rooms, Karla had consulted the fruitful and elegant taste of young Nikolaus, who was to be found there every evening, to which her love of unbridled discord had added a particular, provocative beauty, which corresponded to her personality and which she could not do without. The first time he entered, Nikolaus shook his head in disbelief. The deep tones of the wallpaper were drowned by the blazing scarlet of the door-hangings, and Karla had had the fancy of embroidering a bizarre and restless pattern of blood-red hearts all over his beloved black velvet table-cloths and sofa-covers. But this expression of an uninhibited tem-perament was infectious and compelling. And in the evening, when Karla stood in the glare of the electric lamps, wearing a savage, gypsy-like evening gown which showed off her beautiful breasts and arms, her recalcitrant hair bound with a chain, the wine foaming in the cut-glass goblets tasted all the sweeter and the music had a wonderful, bewitching sound.

But the most exquisite attraction, the one that lured the people there, was Mylada. No one knew where the girl came from, she had never been seen in Prague before, but Karla had discovered her somewhere. She sat in the tavern every evening, her thin face never reddened by the drink. She wore a simple green dress that was like a thin petticoat, revealing her small, pointed breasts. Within a few weeks all the men had fallen in love with her. She had a manner that no one could resist, that seduced the most taciturn of men into conversation and drew out even the most reserved. Her bright eyes, which sometimes clouded over when she was speaking, could captivate the ponderous, intoxicate the fickle and overwhelm the debauched. She was a new and provocative star in the torpid nightlife of the city. Karla had engaged her as a singer, and now and then she would sing a song for the customers in her high voice, accompanied on the piano: German music-hall songs which were popular at the moment, Czech folk-songs such as young men in the working-class districts would play outside on their harmonicas in the evening. But her attraction had nothing to do with these songs.

The unexpected crush of customers made Karla's wine tavern fashionable. A shrill revelry raged there from night until early morning, screaming, stamping and roaring with laughter. Outside in the street, where the arc-lamp burnt, passers-by would stop and then slip enviously into the shadows. When they had passed the tavern, the sweet and sickly verve of the Viennese music called them back and drew their hands to the door-knob. The joie de vivre that was roistering riotously in three-four time from within dug its claws into the lonely and dragged them into the circle of light. And many of Karla's old friends turned up, who had not been together since Dr. Konrad's death. Rušena, the blonde, came, bringing a fat, pockmarked painter along with her. She sat in a corner, supping the vinegary Austrian wine he bought her and gazing into space with a bored smile. It was usually midnight before

Nikolaus appeared. He came from his evening round of dinners and parties in white tie and silk waistcoat, and Karla immediately put a white-stoppered bottle of champagne in the ice-bucket for him.

It was at the end of a very hot day that Severin went with Zdenka to the dark alley for the first time. A grumbling storm was building up over the city and they were both tired. Zdenka was hungry and thirsty, so Severin suggested they should try Karla's. He had seen her adverts in the papers and heard people at the office talking about Mylada. It was still early evening and the tavern was empty. Only old Lazarus was squatting in a corner, drunk. He recognised Severin and waved to him. Next to him Mylada was sitting in her green dress, patiently listening to his chatter. Her bright eyes subjected Zdenka to a cool scrutiny and gave her companion a brief glance. Severin stared, spellbound, at her small, thin face. When he had come in and found the bookseller there he had been gripped by a startled reluctance to stay. Now he was sitting, quiet and transformed, at his table, responding in disbelief to the heavy, tremulous throb of blood in his heart as he watched Mylada. He was puzzled by a strange, oddly familiar expression in her eyes. Zdenka fell into an embarrassed silence when she noticed his furrowed brow and did not dare disturb him. Only when Karla entered and, delighted to see him there, came over to shake his hand, did he wake from his trance and come back to his senses. She sat beside him on the sofa and began to whisper to him about Lazarus. Every evening after he had closed up his shop he came here and got drunk. But he did not stay for long. When the first customers began to appear after the theatres had finished, he went home.

And Karla told him how sometimes when he was drunk he would talk nonsense and cry. 'Sometimes he throws his arms around, like a bird trying to fly and caws like a raven. And then sometimes he screams for his daughter . . .'

Severin went pale. As in a vision he saw in his mind the evening when he had met the Jewess in the dark street and she had sent him packing. He could not remember her words any more, but he could see her body, distended by pregnancy, and

115

he trembled. He stood up and went over to the drunken bookseller.

'Good evening, Lazarus', he said. 'How is Susanna?'

His voice was hoarse with fear, and at the same time he was surprised he had the courage to ask.

The old man stared into his wine without moving his head.

'She came back from the foundling hospital today . . .'

Then, after a long pause, during which the three women looked at each other and held their breath,

'But the child is dead, Master Severin . . . dead as a doornail . . .'

And Lazarus laughed until the tears ran down his gaunt cheeks.

3

The summer became more delightful and tender the closer it came to its end. Every day the sky spread out its immaculate cover and the sun shone down gently. Severin spent his holidays in the city. The mornings, which he could now spend strolling where he pleased, were a delight he had long had to go without. At times the mood of his school holidays, miraculously clear, would seep through the years which had been annihilated by numbing office work, and then all the thoughts of the treadmill crushing his miserable life and of the events of the previous winter would blow away like thin cobwebs. In the early hours, when he was released from sleep, he would stretch his limbs and spend another hour in bed. Reflectively, he watched the rings that the light falling though the meshes of the curtains made on his bedroom door, and felt freed from a burden. Then he washed and went out into the street. He climbed the hill where, from the terraces of Vinohrady one could look down on the valley of Nusle. New, chalk-white buildings gleamed in the sunshine below and the air was filled with the roar of distant railway trains. Somewhere nearby in his childhood had been a small, overgrown garden where he had looked for pebbles and snails' shells and in the spring daisies had grown in the unkempt grass. Beside the Children's Hospital, the dome of Karlov Church peeped out at him like an enormous brown onion and on the other side of the valley rose the new water tower in the fields of Pankrác which always looked to him as if someone had cut it out of a picture book he had possessed as a child. The morning was transparent and shone over the houses. In a factory the whistle of a siren started up and its melancholy voice continued to sound long afterwards in his ear, like a monotonous, avant-garde song.

It was in these morning hours that he first came to appreciate the multifaceted life of the city. Its thousand streets were spread out all around him and when he climbed the slope over there he could see the Moldau flowing past the ramparts of Vyšehrad fortress with the reflections of the sunlight floating on its waters like glowing fires. The grass was sprouting from the crumbling gun embrasures of the rampart walls. Severin thought back to the evenings when he had stood, heavy-hearted and filled with unease, in the maze of houses, quivering with fear and premonitions. The city, as it lay before him, dipping its towers in the morning light, seemed to be more beautiful and yet to have retained its marvels.

On the way home he usually went into some church which had its door open. Since that afternoon on the Kleinseite, there was always something urging him to stand a while in the darkness of the side altars where the earnest-looking statues leant in their niches and the sanctuary lamp burnt in a red glass bowl. He would sit down on a bench and rest for fifteen minutes. At that hour it was rare that anyone else should visit the church, only an occasional old woman shuffling with short steps across the tiles. Severin absorbed the silence like someone who had long been accustomed to noise. In the half-light of the corner he had withdrawn into, his thoughts spun a continuous unbroken thread and entwined his heart in a tangled childhood world. The images of the morning returned as a dream-vision with the waves of the river and the low gables of Hradschin Castle in the dappled air and the blare of the steam-whistle in the valley. Sometimes he was disturbed by a noise when a woman, who had come in quietly, knelt down and started to pray before he turned round. Then he would peer over his shoulder and scrutinise her face.

He gradually came to realise that he was looking for the nun with the starry eyes. On a whim, without foundation as far as he knew, he had christened her Regina and had ended up believing that was her name. He recalled how he had met her under the acacias on the embankment. Some abrupt and unfathomable connection made him think of Mylada.

In such hours he drew up an account for himself of the days on which Zdenka's love had protected him. He experienced everything that had happened to him since then for a second time. What old Lazarus had said came to mind, and futile and

118

cruel tears reminded him of his child. Bit by bit he came to realise that this summer's idyll was a delusion. The sleepy weariness of his heart had made him believe that solace and true happiness had come to stay. But the evil forces still lived there, they proliferated in secret, while he was smiling and kissing Zdenka's lips, and they ate into him like a corrosive acid until his soul was an open sore. Something had disturbed the flickering shadow within him from which he had fled during the winter, and which he recognised again in the dark of the empty church. He did not know whether it was Regina or Mylada, and, strangely, the memories of both intertwined to form a single figure. Susanna's plight was a sign for him that his feet were treading an ominous and ill-fated path. Wherever it led, sorrow and misfortune appeared behind him and joy withered along its track. Concern for Zdenka seized him, and however much he twisted and turned in its claws, he could not free himself from them. And in his frightened love for her he discovered, with an icy shiver, that he took a bitter pleasure in the fact that he held her life in his hands and could crumple it.

When Severin left the church and was back in the open air he shook his head at such fancies. The midday sun flowed like warm honey through the streets and by the wall a blind man was standing with his hat in his hand, blinking. Over the roofs hung the delicious, late-summer heat-haze, that rose from the stubble-fields outside the town. Severin stroked his forehead with his fingers. He continued on his uncertain way and the pleasant numbness of the last few weeks relaxed the tension within him. Sometimes the trill of a canary came from the open window of a ground-floor apartment and from the third floor of one house the scratching of a violin. A humming noise came through the air from a long way off, a metallic ringing that grew stronger and stronger. The midday bells were beginning to sound out from the towers.

4

Nathan Meyer loved to keep his life hidden from people. Since he had opened the tavern in the dark alley together with Karla he had never joined the customers downstairs. He kept his room locked, where he lived among books and pamphlets carelessly scattered over the floor, and he only left it at night, when the other occupants of the building were in bed and he was sure of meeting no one on the stairs. He must have been around forty years old, but his short-cropped hair and smooth-shaven face made him appear much younger. Little was known about his past. His father had owned a large brewery in Russia and had left him a handsome fortune on his death. For years he had lived on the interest on his capital without feeling the need for any kind of activity. His predilection for solitude met with no resistance from his temperament, which was prickly and not softened by any kind of good-naturedness. Some unknown chance had brought him together with Karla, but had had little effect on his way of life. In the apartment they shared his door remained closed to her most of the time. Thus the few people with whom he had some kind of passing relationship found the enthusiasm and persistence with which Nathan suddenly pursued the idea of setting up a tavern astonishing and difficult to understand. Perhaps the stimulus had come from Karla, her active mind seeking something to occupy it in the unbearable monotony of their relationship. But he welcomed her idea with a fanaticism which even Karla, who knew better than anyone else what energies he wasted in his life of idle contemplation, was at a loss to explain. It was he who had tracked down Mylada, rubbing his hands as he insisted she would be a success. But once everything was under way and the business made a promising start, he returned to his old habits and showed no further interest in it.

At least it appeared to be so. For there was no one to see the contented smile on his thin lips when at night the music from the tavern could be heard in his room. The window was open, and Nathan Meyer was sitting at his desk, his head raised, listening. The quiet alley trapped all noises between the high walls of its houses and carried them up to his room. He heard glasses clinking in the tavern below and Mylada's thin laughter inflaming the men. He heard the shrill and ecstatic voices of people getting drunk on wine and conversation. On his smooth face appeared an expression of satisfaction, and he nodded. On some evenings there came from below an uproar lasting for minutes on end, the hiss and gurgle of unbridled lust bubbling over and turning somersaults in its inability to contain itself. Torrid chords on the piano sounded through the noise and heavy fingers rummaged through the keys, extracting rapturous melodies, waltzes and marches. Then Nathan Meyer would take his hat and coat from the wardrobe and go down the stairs. Unseen and unrecognised he would wait beside the tavern, counting the customers who disappeared through its doors. The arc-light painted a bright circle in the darkness of the alley and its glaring white beam illuminated the faces of the guests as they entered. For just a second Nathan could see the souls of the people as, dazzled, they paused outside the door and waited for a moment. The lamp shone more deeply into the faces, through the daytime veils, revealing the hollows fear had dug into them, the furrows and fissures round reddened eyes. Nathan had pulled his hat down over his forehead and turned up the collar of his coat. He stood motionless in the darkness, guarding the house.

Severin remembered Nathan Meyer from the day Dr. Konrad had been buried. In his mind he could see the tall, broad-boned figure with the irate mouth standing next to Karla among the mourners in the cold twilight of the winter afternoon. A sympathetic concern had stirred within him for the woman who had been his lover until a short while ago; beside the robust shoulders of the man her svelte elegance curled back in on itself in weary abandon. Since then he had not come across him at all, not even later when Karla had moved in with him and the tavern in the dark alley was already in operation. It was in a small coffee house near the Moldau that he saw Nathan Meyer again. He had taken to visiting the place before going to bed whenever he had spent the evening with Zdenka and his murderous and cowardly night thoughts kept him from going home. Recently he had felt the need to spend at least an hour alone with his thoughts after he had left Zdenka and her gentle caresses were no longer there to calm the restlessness which was beginning to draw its ever-tightening noose around him. His holidays were coming to an end. Autumn, sombre and constricting, was waiting for him. His silent existence in the office would begin again, where the days were like walls, one beside the other, chafing his life in the narrow gaps between them. When Zdenka was with him and he could feel the warmth of her hand on his arm and hear her beautiful voice telling him of the great happiness of their love, then he would walk beside her with the expression of one who has been nursed back to health. His malaise returned to him together with the mist that now descended on the early morning streets, prophesying the end of summer. As he had done at the beginning, he found himself again looking down with a twisted smile on Zdenka's blond hair while she snuggled up to him. When she had gone to bed and the light in her window went out, he dug his teeth into the flesh of his fingertips. He walked through the city and the street lamps traced his shadow on the paving stones behind him. In the coffee house he sat by the window and pushed the curtain aside. The gigantic rump of the Rudolfinum Museum stood out against a night sky in which the late summer stars were burning embers, like red Chinese lanterns.

It was on one such night that Severin got into conversation with Nathan Meyer. The latter had been watching him for some time from behind the newspaper he was reading and a thoughtful expression drew the corners of his lips down even farther as his long fingers tapped the ash from his cigarette into the brass ash-tray. At first Severin's response was morose and taciturn. He felt uncomfortable and it irritated him that Meyer was steadily scrutinising his face. But it was not long before he was sitting spellbound, listening to this man's spontaneous confession. They were alone in the low room of the coffee house, with only the heavy breathing of the sleeping waiter coming from one corner and, from the card-room, the thump of an ace being played. Strange revelations were made. Nathan's voice blazed with the blind, spiteful fury of the solitary and seethed with the poison that ravages the hearts of cripples and lunatics: hatred of the world. His wet lips quivered from the depths of his soul as he spoke, preaching an angry refusal to believe in the goodness and glory of the earth with the unmitigated, arrogant scorn of a damned soul. He leant over to Severin with his dry, rasping whisper,

'There is a bit of the chemist in all of us who come from Russia. At home I have bombs and devices enough to demolish a whole street, if I wanted. But that is only something for the amateur. There are better, more subtle means, that are allowed by law, that the authorities license. Have you ever been to my tavern?'

An icy shiver ran down Severin's spine. He looked into Nathan's cunning, grey eyes and could suddenly understand him without further explanation. He was seized with terror of the man who went hunting souls without anyone noticing.

'A week ago a young man shot himself,' the Russian went on. 'He stole money from the bank where he worked, to drink my champagne and sleep with Mylada. I went to see his corpse in the Institute of Pathology; a mere slip of a lad, scarcely over twenty. His mother had a stroke when she heard about it – and that is only the beginning. I know them all, those who go to the bar. I watch them when they think they are unobserved, from the dark shadow by the door.'

Then after a pause, as Severin waited in silence, 'I have found a name for the place, a good name that will attract people: *The Spider*.'

Severin stood up. There was a bitter taste at the back of his throat and he felt dizzy. Nathan's cropped head disappeared in the smoke of his cigarette and for a second Severin saw an image that made him catch his breath: it was the city with deep streets and a thousand windows; and in the middle was the tavern in the dark alley. The lamp over the entrance was like a staring eye and people were thronging round the door. They came one after the other, like midges round a light. Inside sat Mylada in her green dress. Invisible, huddled up beneath the curving legs of the piano, crouched an ungainly being that the people of the night called Pleasure . . .

Severin shook himself and the picture disappeared.

'Wouldn't you like to see my laboratory some time?' he heard Nathan Meyer ask.

'I don't know', he replied, and had to cling on to the back of the chair to stop himself from falling.

5

The rainy days came, washing away the last traces of summer. There were great pools of water on the paths in the parks and the leaves that the wind tore from the trees stuck to the benches. The cabs drove round the city with soggy leather roofs and boys splashed barefoot through the puddles and built dams out of mud by the edge of the pavement. From the damp sky dusk fell more quickly than usual at this time of the year.

Severin stood by his window. Slowly, by fits and starts, the sparse life of the district where he lived wended its way through the afternoon. A coal-cart rumbled over the cobbles and the huge horses hung their heads morosely. A man scurried along the houses, the cloth of his black umbrella gleaming in the wet. Here and there a grubby paper kite flew up into the air, dragged on its string through the rain by some child; then it would start a clumsy, anxious fluttering and tumble to the ground. The bell on the door of the corner shop jangled; a young woman with frizzed locks over her forehead came out to look at the weather. Then she lifted up her skirts so that her pretty legs could be seen right up to the knees, and ran down the street.

Severin recalled the autumn rains of his childhood. It was all just like today and his boyhood desires dredged a doleful yearning from his heart. The bell of the shop opposite his father's house had had the same ring. Severin waited impatiently for the door to be opened again. Once, as a very small child before he went to school, he had been ill with pneumonia. Sometimes during the illness a strange feeling had crept over him as he lay at home in bed with the light from the street slanting across the flowers painted on the ceiling. His mother was busy in the kitchen and from somewhere came the drone of a barrel organ. The fever had gnawed a round spot that felt soft and was covered with a fine membrane. A comparison occurred to him: he remembered the sweets that he used to buy at the market for a copper; as tne sugar melted in his mouth the liquid centre felt soft to the tongue under a paper-thin skin. It was a sensation which seemed to have left him for good long ago. Now it returned, clear and distinct, and Severin recognised it again. At the same time a swarm of familiar images, that had faded with time, surfaced within him; he had forgotten them, and the rainy day swept them back into his memory: the sooty balcony with the iron railings where he invented childish games with his brother and shot at the cats in the garden with his catapult; old Julinka, whom his parents still provided for and who had to scrub the splintery wooden stairs in return; the summer evenings by the open door when the red clouds between the roofs had brought his first, uncomprehended tears and the maids in the neighbouring yards had sung the Czech folk-songs, whose banal sweetness still moved him even now.

Mylada knew those songs too.

Severin leant his head against the smooth pane. A wheedling pain twisted his lips into a sob.

Night had come, transforming the rain into a dripping fog which squeezed through the gaps in the windows and and gave the sleepers uneasy dreams. Severin could not stand it in the house any longer. He had not been out since midday and stabbing cramps set the blood throbbing at his temples. He had made Zdenka wait in vain today and an irritating feeling of remorse had built up in his mind, like the mist veiling the gas-lamps outside. He threw his waterproof round his shoulders and pulled the hood over his hat.

On the market square of the district where he lived he surprised two figures who were embracing behind the empty fruit-stalls. Severin stood and watched them until the man noticed him and fled into the darkness with the girl. He was seized with an overpowering yearning for the simple happiness of these people. With dull and brooding concentration he tried for the hundredth time to discover what had led him off the beaten track of life into this desolate wilderness. And he was suddenly consumed with a painful, impotent lust, oppressed with fear and torn by doubt, for the kiss of the

126

woman who had inflamed his desire at the very same moment when Lazarus had told him of the death of his child.

He stopped by the ramp leading up to the Museum. Below him stretched Wenceslas Square and the autumn mists hung in white clouds between the electric lights. Severin flung out his arms.

'Mylada!' he cried, and his voice fluttered through the mist like a trembling bird.

In the Spider the hands of the wall-clock had already reached the twelfth hour. The bar was packed and the provocative smell of spilt wine floated over the tables. Laughter climbed up the green smoke-rings from the cigars and fell back to the floor with a squawk. The noise of the conversations grew to an irrepressible roar that broke off with a gurgle whenever the music started up or one of the customers began to sing in a loud voice. Karla herself sat at the piano in a colourful and seductive outfit. As she played, she bent her beautiful head back until it touched the nape of her neck.

Severin sat behind her and ordered a bottle. He choked on the thick, reeking air of the room and sweat broke from every pore, making his shirt stick to his skin. Karla played any tune her guests requested. Her fingers sent the spurious drivel of operetta warbling round the room and the scent of her body fizzed in their throats with the wine and scorched through their veins. A senseless, reckless exuberance was rollicking inside their heads and swamping their hearts. Mylada detached herself from a group of very young men in tails with white cummerbunds. Her thin lips laughed with an infinite promise of pleasure as she leant over Severin.

'Give me a drink', she said, holding out her glass.

He watched her tongue as it darted out between her sharp teeth, and had to keep a hold on himself not to kiss her. He put his arm round her and pulled her down onto his lap.

'I have already seen those eyes before. Have you a sister, Mylada?'

'I had a sister who looked very much like me, but she died.'

Severin stroked the hair back from her face; she did not

stop him and she clasped him with her legs. Her body was as small as a child's and her breasts jutted out under her thin dress.

'Come to me tonight', he whispered, and she replied:

'She was called Regina. She was a nun.'

6

Severin had stopped counting time since Mylada had become his mistress. The days coalesced into one single, richly coloured, blazing mirage, flooding everything with its dazzling light. Everything that had had meaning for him, everything that had depressed or excited him, disappeared out of his life as if it had never existed. With the carefree assurance of a sleep-walker, he carried out the activities which gave shape to his existence. He did his work in the office without feeling the strain which normally burdened these hours. He no longer felt the furtive and malicious hatred of the things that used to offend him, he only had room within himself for the boundless self-indulgence of his love. Never would he have believed a woman could make him feel the things he felt each day. Rapturous depths opened up before him in which he submerged his wild and bewildered senses and his paralysed soul.

Mylada understood his body. With the shrewd and experienced intuition of her depraved youth, she grasped his nature and submitted to every whim she could discover there. She uncovered the secret recesses of his desires and pursued them to the roots of his nerves. She taught him her bizarre and unbridled love-games and intoxicated him with her caresses. Her kisses were inventive and the joy they brought him was a sinful and despairing lasciviousness. Often, when her arms were round his neck and her eyes clouded with lust, he lost all sense of the present. The room where they were seemed strange, foreign, and the lamp by his bed gave a peculiar light. He saw the sparks dancing beneath Mylada's eyelids and a golden wave washed all thoughts out of his mind.

Her weak and fragile body had an unsuspected power of love within it. There was a passion in her which she squandered without restraint, which clung to Severin and exhausted him. Women had always been a disappointment to him. His experiences with them had always lacked that great, compelling force, that could overwhelm him and dictate to him, that was irresistible and deadly. For the first time a lightning-bolt struck his life, crushing it and bathing it in light. At times a memory approached him unasked, and Zdenka's image appeared and pleaded. At night, when he suddenly woke from sleep and stared at the darkness, it came to him and tried to save him. Then once more the sheen of her blond hair ensnared his heart and the sound of a voice came to him like a far-off bell. But the next day led him back to Mylada and her lips made him forget everything else.

When the afternoon came, and the fine spray of the October shadows hung on the walls, he sat at home and waited. The street noises sounded unclear and changed, and the passing carts made the floorboards tremble. Sometimes there was a roaring and a thudding in his head which frightened him and which he could not get rid of. He held his hands over his ears and realised that it came from within and that the noise was inside him. An anxious alarm burrowed its fingers into his intestines. Then the doorbell rang and Mylada came into his room and took off her coat.

He loved everything that belonged to her. Every dress that she wore on her fiery body became a fetish. He tried to reawaken her breath from the meshes of a veil she once left behind in his apartment, and the odour of the gloves that he stole from her comforted him in the hours when he did not possess her. When, with cruelly lingering fingers, she undressed before him, the destiny which he could no longer escape and to which he bowed the knee, threw him at her feet. Sobbing, tormented by an rapture beyond this world, he brushed his lips against her petticoat.

He knew that when he left Zdenka for Mylada he had sacrificed her once and for all. It was too late to turn back, and the notion that there had been a time that was not full to overflowing with this love that was consuming him, was a pale wraith of a thought. Often, when he took her in his arms and she curled up in his lap like a naughty child, he saw, looking at him from beneath her eyelashes, the eyes of the nun he had knelt beside in the church in the summer. He told Mylada about the meeting and how she had smiled when he had spoken the Salve Regina beside her. Mylada laughed and began to talk about her sister, who had been dead for years, so that he must have been seeing a ghost. But Severin refused to accept it and stuck by his story. The white face of the young woman who had knelt by his side was clear and real in his mind, and the sultry fire of sinful desire she had set off still smouldered inside him.

Mylada allowed him his fantasies. With the delicate instinct which she used to dominate men, she soon realised that they concealed a source of new and complex pleasures which she felt compelled to open up and taste. One day she arrived later than usual, when the room was already darkening in the autumn dusk. Feverish, exhausted by expectation, he opened the door. Before him, calm and wordless, her hands crossed piously over her breast, stood the young nun, just as he had seen her under the acacias on the embankment. Her limbs were enveloped in the wide flowing folds of her habit and under the black hood gleamed the same starry eyes.

'Regina!' he stammered.

She fell on him with a cry of delight and her lips sucked at his mouth. It was her kisses that told him it was Mylada. He ripped open the coarse cloth of her habit, under which her flesh shimmered like beautiful matt silk. He grabbed her by the belt and carried her to his bed.

'Regina! Regina!'

A miraculous joy beyond anything in the world ran through his veins like boiling metal and burnt a sweet, coral-red brand into his poor heart overwhelmed by love.

From now on Severin spent the nights that followed these afternoons in the Spider. Separated from the rest, he sat in his place and watched the customers courting Mylada. For each one she had a word, a bright note in her voice, a whispered promise that each thought was for him alone and that brought a surreptitious flush to his cheeks. But in between her glance flew back to Severin, and when she passed him her fingers stroked his hair. She looked at him when she sang the songs he loved, the songs that had an echo of the music of his childhood. She too had the swaying, soulful grace of Slav women which had attracted him to Zdenka. But she also had a dangerous nimbleness, a cunning sentimentality, which clung to the surface and did not demystify her being. Severin drank the dark red wine Karla poured for him and sat there, motionless. He took no share in the merriment which pressed itself upon him, and it did not rouse him from his absorption. In the middle of the mad exuberance of the rest he was alone with Mylada and his secret thoughts of the hour when she would next belong to him alone.

It was already light when he drained his glass and went out into the street. A man with a pole over his shoulder was in front of him, turning off the last street-lamps. A gaggle of gossiping women passed him carrying huge baskets on their backs. They were stall–holders taking vegetables to the early market. Without getting undressed he stretched out on his bed to sleep.

One morning, as the door of the tavern was bolted behind him, he found Nathan Meyer standing beside him. His thin lips twisted in a mocking smile as he greeted him and walked some way down the alley with him. He cleared his throat uneasily and shook his head as he said goodbye.

'She's a bitch!' he said several times through his teeth, and Severin could not tell whether it expressed satisfaction, or a warning.

With a strange, almost fatherly expression, the Russian looked him in the eyes.

'She's a bitch, Severin! Believe me, she's a bitch!'

7

His love for Mylada had appeared in Severin's life like a tongue of fire abruptly shooting up from the conflagration and casting its ghastly light on the darkness around. Now, after a few weeks during which she had abandoned herself perversely to a caprice, she turned away from him, leaving him to the icy shades once more, and he was enveloped in a terrible and lonely horror. The fires of passion had burnt out his soul, leaving nothing but an empty shell. He could not understand that he was alone once more, that all that was left of the blaze were ashes, and the pain of ugly, flickering, festering sores. With the frenzy of one who is completely lost, he rebelled against fate.

Every day he waited in his room for her to come. The hands on the grandfather clock creaked past each quarter and hours passed. Mylada did not come any more. He fell face down to the ground, and blood and spittle flowed from his distorted mouth, soaking the carpet.

At night in the tavern he grabbed her arm. He dug in his fingernails down to the bone so that she staggered and called for help and bit furiously at his wrist, tearing the skin to shreds. Finally, she managed to pull herself away.

'I don't want to! It's all over!'

Racked with disgust, he fled into the street. A gust of wind took his hat away, but he ignored it. Bare-headed, crushed by misery, he ran through the darkness, and the looming figure of terror pursued him, and there was no escape. A policeman's uniform glinted beside him and a voice barked a command. Severin swore in reply and ran on.

He stopped in the fields beyond the last suburb. His breath rattled in his throat and his veins throbbed, threatening to burst at his neck. He tore open his collar and gradually managed to collect himself. The clouds drifting across the sky parted for a while, exposing the moon. Severin recognised the place where he was. There was a ruined farm nearby where no one had lived for some time. In the summer tramps slept inside its fissured walls and by day the occasional rag-and-bone-man would search through the old garbage to see if there was anything left worth having.

A few paces farther on, the footpath joined the road. The huge, newly built factories towered up along it and beyond them began the cemeteries. Severin had not been here since the death of Dr. Konrad. His thoughts went through the days that had passed since the funeral, picking their frightened and fragmented way round reality. The moon disappeared and darkness coagulated over the fields. Severin continued on his way, turning his back on the murky lights of the city and leaving them farther and farther behind. The night wind combed his hair and fingered his naked chest through his open shirt. His blood stopped its raging and calmed down. Behind the wrought-iron gate of the churchyard was the tree beside Konrad's grave which had once pursued him, even into his sleep. Severin laughed as he passed. He took a clump of earth and threw it over the wall.

Weariness clutched at his legs with a timorous arm. He thought of the farm by the road. He wanted to sleep, and if he could find a corner there to hide in until morning he would not have to go back to the city. He suddenly remembered that only recently the newspapers had been talking about the farm. There had been a suicide and the corpse of an army officer had been found amongst the rubble. Severin had known him, he had been a regular at the Spider. He recalled the evening when Karla had brought the news of his death to the tavern. At that time he had not concerned himself with it; love had churned up his soul and stopped up his eyes and ears. Now he could see the connection clearly. A wretched hatred, covered in boils, erupted within him; he raised his arm and shook his fist at the darkness.

The days following that night brought Severin's collapse. The tough vital force which he possessed, and which had withstood all his debauchery and crises, crumbled and broke under the pressure of a sadness beyond hope. He went sick and did not return to the office. He found it impossible to think or do anything that was not connected with the self-tormenting pleasure he took in his pain and which he kept on reliving from start to finish. After hours of self-absorbed apathy, he would be gripped by a merciless and uncouth anger. Then he would foam at the mouth and stifle his horrible cries in the pillows. He clenched his fists and shattered the glass of the mirror that showed him his forehead covered in peeling skin and his eyes reddened from lack of sleep. He avoided people who cautiously turned round and looked at him in the street and recognised the grey face with the swollen bags under the eyes.

That was how he was when Nathan Meyer found him one evening outside the Spider. He was staring into the circle of light thrown by the lamp over the door and his teeth were chattering when Meyer came up to him and put his hand on his shoulder.

'Don't go back in there', he said.

His voice was soft, with that tender and firm tone adults use when talking to children.

'Never go back in there, Severin!'

Then he took him by the arm and led him up the stairs to his room. Severin followed unresisting.

'What do you want from me, Nathan?' was all he asked, leaning his weakened body against the tall man.

Nathan Meyer turned up the lamp and pulled up a chair for his guest. In front of him he put a box of those long and slim cigarettes which he had sent from Russia and which he chain-smoked himself.

'Light a cigarette', he commanded.

Then he began to pace up and down the room. Severin sat and listened. It was the same tirade he had heard in the coffee house, all those weeks ago. His agitation chopped his sermon up into short sentences as he preached war against the world. But there was something else his words betrayed: friendly sympathy and unconcealed concern which Severin could not understand and which he found strangely touching, coming from those lips.

'What do you want from me?' he asked again.

Nathan Meyer stood in front of him.

'I like you, Severin.'

He leant down with a smile.

'You are one of us! One of the brotherhood!'

'The brotherhood? What brotherhood?'

But there was no answer to his question. Meyer jangled his key-ring and opened his desk.

'You can be having a look at the things in there while I go downstairs for a bottle of wine. But watch your cigarette.'

Curious, Severin stood up and pulled open the heavy drawer. Nathan Meyer had left him on his own, and he was visited by a strange feeling in this room with bookshelves covering the walls right up to the ceiling and the lamplight flickering on old furniture. In the drawer, carefully stacked one next to the other, were iron high-explosive bombs in all shapes and sizes, spherical hand-grenades, egg-shaped or square canisters with white fuses.

Severin bent over the open drawer. A bright-red thought shuffled its lascivious way through his brain and his hands trembled against his cuffs. He gave each bomb a discriminating scrutiny. There was one, a medium-sized, oddly shaped thing, which lay amongst the others like a black heart. Severin picked it up and stuffed it in his pocket.

'Well?' asked Meyer as he came back into the room with a full carafe and two glasses.

When Severin remained silent he murmured contemptuously, 'Children's toys', and locked the drawer.

'Come on, let's drink a glass to the brotherhood.'

8

After weeks of cruelly abandoned solitude Severin could no longer control his desire to see Mylada again. The pale, anaemic visions which his imagination made appear before him and which he followed in the shadow of the night kept on leading him back to the place where the light from the tavern lamp fell on the street like a huge, dazzling wheel. The echo of Meyer's warning had long since died away in his soul. One evening, doubled up with shame and ravaged by longing, he was back in the Spider.

He could no longer bring himself to forgo the last and sharpest thorn in his suffering flesh. Mylada ignored him, as if he were some unknown customer. But he used the lascivious twist of her voice and the cunning glint of gold in her pupils to rekindle the memory of her passion and her pernicious and corrupting love. He called back the memory of the time when she had come to him dressed as a nun. He shuddered and sighed under her kisses and held in rapturous embrace a ghost that had once bewildered him in the summer, under the acacias.

Now he sat amongst the others with his elbows on the table. He held his hands over his face and through his fingers he watched Mylada laugh with the men and he rediscovered the lines of her body under her dress. Lazarus, the bookseller, was rocking her on his knees. His bald head was pressing against her breasts and Severin could see the furrows of his cranium under the taut skin. He recalled the evening when he had gone through the city armed with a rock in order to kill someone. Mylada was playing with his beard, which hung down from the old man's jaw, sparse and unkempt, and her bright eyes clouded over in a way that was so familiar. A feeling of disgust slithered up into his throat like a slimy fist. He drained his glass and left.

Outside, the winter had spread its deep and inexhaustible

night sky over the city. Nowhere was there a star to be seen and the departing autumn was dragging a tacky, ice-cold trail of vapour behind it over the cobblestones. A tiny lamp was smoking by the mobile urn of a tea-vendor; two prostitutes in feather hats and bright-yellow summer coats having a quick bite to eat were talking and laughing. Severin went up and bought some cigarettes. One of the girls spoke to him and begged for a copper. He took a handful of silver out of his pocket and gave it to her.

He was in the grip of an apathetic and detached austerity. He did not know where to go, nor what to do. From the carpeted entrance to a bar came a warm blast with the smell of cheap spirits and the commissionaire raised his hand to his cap in salute. Severin thought of the years when he had spent his life in such places. He was overcome with a gnawing longing for those days. Then he had had a place of refuge. He had not been alone in his wretched, narrow existence; simple desires had kept him company, a lachrymose presentiment of the bewildering grandeur of the world. Now he knew better. Debilitated and filthy, ravaged and worn out, he was about to expire amidst the garbage, just because a nightclub hostess had sent him packing.

Now he could understand Nathan Meyer's talk. There were people for whom the glory of life was nothing but marsh fire: cynics with an unlucky touch, pariahs hounded through the streets by abject fear, murderers, men with the mark of Cain. That was the brotherhood to which Severin now belonged.

He had always sensed it, even when as a boy he had read his book of wild adventures and longed for his own. The pale flames of his worm-eaten youth had always given off a reddish smoke that came from the foul recesses of his heart. The happiness others enjoyed had always seemed like a children's picture-puzzle to him. He had played blindly with fate and had stumbled past its miserable mouse-traps without harming himself.

He looked up and saw that he had been walking in a circle. He could see the little lamp beside the urn glowing, and the

man's white apron shone in the darkness. Severin suppressed a
sob. That man had a home to go to and the candle-end
behind the broken glass burnt with a peaceful light.

And himself, Severin?

He felt a pain deep within his innermost soul. The sweet
image of a woman, buried beneath rubbish and debris, raised a
sorrowful face towards him. But he threw back his head and
refused to see it.

Or . . . ? Was it possible?

His limbs gave way under a mild and shaming weakness. By
the steps of a house entrance he sank to his knees and cooled
his brow on the stones. He folded his hands and shut his eyes,
and just above him, in the narrow strip of sky between the
houses, a shy star appeared, radiant.

A thin, pale-grey light was announcing the dawn when
Severin pulled himself up and set off in the direction of the
Old Town Square. The fleeting outlines of the colourful
posters were already visible on the walls and the man with the
urn was getting ready to go home. Outside the chemist's in
the square a bleary-eyed young woman was leaning against
the wall, tugging at the bell.

Sleepily, the concierge held out his sweaty hand to him and
nodded in satisfaction when he recognised the late visitor.
Severin gave him a coin and made his way up the stairs to
Zdenka's apartment. For an endless moment his heart stopped
beating before he knocked on the door.

A sound came from within.

'Is someone there?' asked a voice.

'It's me, Severin.'

The door opened and a hot hand drew him into the room.
The paraffin lamp with the green shade was smoking on the
table. Zdenka was in her nightdress. Her hair fell in blond
ringlets to her neck and she shivered with cold.

'Why have you come?' she asked in a calm voice. Severin
took off his hat and held it in his hands. He glanced round,
taking in the whole room in one long farewell look. The early
morning light was trickling in through the curtains and making the glow of the lamp seem thin and shabby. Beside the bed

was the cupboard where Zdenka kept her clothes and under-wear. The purple china vase on the chest was cracked and the colour had faded from the handle. There was a bunch of withered flowers in it that they had gathered together in the woods, one day in the summer.

Zdenka looked at him and waited. Her nightdress was slipping down over her naked breasts and she hunched her shoulders with the cold. He stretched his arms out in a rehearsed, mechanical gesture. Then he dropped them again.

'Why have you come?'

He turned and went out of the door.

9

The wind, which had spent the morning hours rattling the shopkeepers' signs, had gone to rest. A calm evening brought a clear sky, and a beautiful, pale sun began to shine. Severin sat up in his rumpled bed and looked at the clock. The long rest after a sleepless night had not strengthened him. He washed the hot daze from his eyes and dressed carefully.

Along the street he met groups of adolescent schoolboys who were making their way home and talking animatedly to each other. Severin turned to watch them with a vague feeling of envy. The change in the weather had lured people out of their houses and a throng was strolling along the pavements and gathering outside the shop windows. Girls with becoming velvet bonnets on hair done up in a pert style pushed their way through the crowd. A pair of lovers stood at the cross-roads admiring the sunset. Streaks of poppy-red appeared along the edge of the roofs, setting the chimneys on fire. A fat cloud suddenly burst into flame and sailed across Charles Square like a huge lump of gold foil.

Severin made his way in leisurely fashion, with a cold and determined curiosity. He was ambushed by the shadowy feeling which always came to haunt him when he had been exhausted and to which he abandoned himself without resistance. His consciousness split off and took on independent existence outside him. The past and the present rolled past him like pictures in a cyclorama and, bewildered and submissive, he was a spectator of his own life. The faces of the people walking beside him, the outlines of the houses that he knew, were invested with a new and special vividness which aroused his attention.

At the corners of the side-streets the chestnut vendors had set up their stoves. A warm radiance had settled over the city. A shrivelled old woman on crutches was hobbling laboriously across the road. Outside the doorways, long-haired students were chatting to maidservants and the blue twilight enticed cosy shadows from every corner. An early lamp glittered out-side the Church of the Knights of St. Francis, filling the air with glassy colours.

Severin went onto the bridge. There was a cool breeze from the water which blew away the mood to which he had abandoned himself. Memory reappeared, sharp as a razor, tearing to shreds the veil of delusion woven by his senses. The evening fluttered over the river. A motor car with milky-white headlamps gave a melancholy toot and the bell of the little chapel at the foot of the Castle Steps was sounding the angelus. Severin walked past the black stone statues on the parapet. He bit into his tongue and the blood flowed in his mouth, tasting like gall. This was not the city he knew. This was a peepshow with respectable citizens going about their business and St. John Nepomuk guarding the Moldau with hypocritical hands.

Twilight was thickening as Severin passed through the Bridge Tower leading to the Kleinseite near where the monu-ment to Field Marshal Radetzky stood. Outside the gate of the main police station a soldier was marching up and down with a rifle over his shoulder, and the square with the leafy arcades was tinted like a yellowed copper engraving. Severin climbed Spornergasse to the Hradschin. The city he knew was different. Its streets led one astray and ill fortune lurked on the thresholds. Damp, treacherous walls set one's heart beat-ing, the night crept past blank windows, suffocating the soul in sleep. Satan had his traps set everywhere, in the churches and in the houses of the courtesans. His breath was in their mur-derous kisses and in the nuns' habits he went on the prowl.

Outside the entry to the Castle courtyard Severin turned his head. Night had fallen and Prague was spread out at his feet with its brimming lights.

Somewhere a dog howled and its apprehensive barking sounded as if it came from the depths, from some long-forgotten shaft in the ground beneath the crooked alleys of the Hradschin . . .

In the Spider a large company had been gathered since the

early evening. Lazarus was treating everyone to champagne. Mylada's birthday was being celebrated with obscene jokes.

Among them were many acquaintances from the group that used to meet in Dr. Konrad's apartment. Lazarus had invited them all, even Nikolaus was there, sitting among them with a serious, bored expression, and the pock-marked painter who was living with the fair-haired Rušena now. Mylada was sitting at the head of the table in all her capricious fascination. Her supple shamelessness delighted the men and exhilarated the younger folk. One after the other drank to her and she dipped her red tongue into each single glass. Lust danced like a flame across their faces and fumbled at her green dress. Somebody suggested a raffle, the proceeds from which should be drunk as soon as possible; amid cheers and laughter Mylada declared she would sleep with the winner. The price of the tickets was high, but in spite of that all but one had been sold when Severin entered to be greeted by loud hallos.

Mylada welcomed him.

'Do you want the last raffle ticket?'

She held the scrap of white paper between her fingertips.

'What can I win?' he asked.

'Me!'

Without a word he put all the money he had left into her hands and took the ticket.

The draw began. The numbers were put in an ice-bucket and they all pressed shouting round the table; they were all in the grip of a furious excitement. Their foreheads were reddened with wine and intoxication gave a grotesque tautness to their features, turning them into the faces of beasts or gargoyles.

Mylada was blindfolded and took a ticket from the ice-bucket. There was silence in the room as she unfolded the paper.

'You're in luck, Severin', she said with a grin.

There was an envious pause.

Severin approached. The blood was pounding in his ears and he was pale. He held up the object he had stolen from

Nathan Meyer's desk not long ago. Like a white worm, the fuse twisted round his arm.

'A bomb!' someone exclaimed and everyone shuddered at the shriek of terror.

'I came to kill you . . .'

His voice cracked. Red-eyed, he stared at the lamp.

Nikolaus took the bomb out of his hand and stroked his cheeks, as if he were a child.

Why?' he asked tenderly.

'Because I hate you!'

'And why didn't you do it?' whispered Mylada, looking up at him, her lips apart. She straightened up and her breasts brushed against him.

'I've won the raffle!'

A deathly shame threw him to the ground. He knelt down and put his head in her lap. He was overcome with sobbing and he cried. But the laughter of the drunken crowd flowed over him, transforming his tears into filthy, searing mud.

The Ghost of the Jewish Ghetto

'The Ghost of the Jewish Ghetto' was one of many evocations of old Prague written by Paul Leppin. It was first published in 'Der Sturm', 1914/15,

Only ten years ago, in the middle of Prague, where today tall, airy apartment blocks form wide boulevards, stood the Jewish quarter: a squint, gloomy jumble of nooks and crannies from which no storm was strong enough to blow away the smell of mould and damp masonry and where, in summer, the open doors exhaled a poisonous miasma. Filth and poverty each outstank the other, and the eyes of the children that grew up there had a dull, cruel glint of depravity. Alleys would sometimes pass under low, vaulted viaducts through the belly of a house, or they would suddenly twist to one side to come to an abrupt end at a blind wall. The sharp-faced junk dealers, who piled up their wares on the bumpy cobbles outside their shops, would accost passers-by. Girls with painted lips leant against the house entrances, full of coarse laughter, whispering in the men's ears and lifting up their skirts to show their yellow or lime-green stockings. Ancient, slack-jawed bawds, their hair streaked with white, shouted from the windows, hammered, waved and gurgled with gratified zeal when a man took the bait and came closer.

Fornication had made its home here, and in the evening its red lamps lured men in. There were streets where every building was a house of ill repute, low dives where vice shared its bed with hunger, where consumptive women carried on a meagre trade with their withered charms, secret chambers where villainy, with whispers and sly winks, violated school-age girls and sold their helpless, bewildered innocence for a few pieces of tarnished silver. There were smart, luxuriously furnished taverns where one's foot sank into the carpets and where well-fed, voluptuous whores strutted about in long silk gowns.

Not far from the synagogue, beside the squalid shacks of Gypsy Lane, was a two-storey building which housed the *Salon Aaron*. In this seedy environment it had an almost well-cared-for look, in spite of the fact that part of the plaster was crumbling from the walls and the dust and rain had smeared gaudy stripes across the blind windows. By day it was quiet; only rarely did a customer slip up the worn steps into the dark vestibule, to emerge an hour later, furtively, his coat-collar turned up around his ears. But at night here loud, bright, quivering life welled up from some secret spring. The windows glowed, and inside, the laughter fluttered round like a bird trapped in a cage.

Johanna's laughter was part of it. It was a hot, throaty purring, that rubbed itself up against you; it could be clearly distinguished from the voices of the other girls, and sometimes it would even echo through the morning silence like a happy, infatuated lark. Johanna was happy because the men came to her. They desired her more than her colleagues because she gave each and every one of them something of the fearful, tormenting, restless sweetness which filled her and which was absent from the lethargic bodies of the others. Their profession, which to the other women in the house seemed a boring, irksome chore, aroused within her an ecstatic yearning for love, was a spur she could feel goading her flesh and which brought a virginal lustre to her eyes. With lips that were cracked and sore from kissing, she would slake this thirst on the mouths of men, again and again imbued with the bridal ecstasy that had accompanied her first lovemaking. In the intervals afforded by her promiscuous activity – and unbearably long and lonely they seemed to her – she listened for the steps of the passers-by outside the house, and when the bell over the door jingled, she would flush and sigh. There were often days when she enjoyed the delights of love until she was sated with it; but as she lay in bed, with heavy head and aching limbs, her mind went back to this lover and then to that one, savouring the memory, luxuriating in it, and she would smile in the darkness. Sometimes, especially in the summer, when she finally made her way to her bed in the last hours before morning, her restlessness would turn into torment. Then she would go to the open window in her nightdress and look down onto the Jewish quarter. She would stretch out her bare arms, feeling the warm rain like drops of blood on her skin. The streets below were where she belonged: the ghetto where the sleepy lights of the brothels twinkled, where bulky shadows crouched in sordid alleyways, whilst in the distance the whine of a violin or the harsh tinkling of the Pianolas were making one last effort to entice revellers. A rapturous melancholy bathed her face in tears. Tenderly, the night wind fondled her breasts, and she would let her head fall back and her lips would purse in a kiss.

In the evenings, beneath the festive lights of the *Salon Aaron*, as the wine-glasses chinked on the marble tables, she would dance to the music. The sensuality that she suffered from made her limbs soft and relaxed, goading her, skirts swirling, into an urgent abandon that suffused her rigid features with a strange beauty which was more provocative, more enticing, than all the wiles of the other women. She danced alone or with the customers. Her slim figure would bend back in the arms of her partners, press up against them insistently, tremble and shiver; and if one had danced with the blonde Johanna, he was sure to go up to her room with her as well. Her lips were greedy and feverish. The more men that found their way to her door, the more unbridled was the lust with which she fell upon them; her desire had the power to move men and leave them dazed; her passion was a willing instrument that could blaze up into sheer bliss.

Then came the day when disease demanded its penance from her body. It welled up from the decaying walls of the ghetto, from its debauched streets, and poisoned her kisses. It burnt up her blood and made her veins dry and cracked; it choked the laughter and the amorous murmurs in her throat; it disfigured her body with red blotches and dragged her through the gauntlet of the vituperation of the foul-mouthed whores to the fear and trembling of the hospital. There she lay in a hot bed, and the thoughts fell from the ceiling onto her forehead like heavy drops. She thought of the women who were sitting at that moment in the *Salon Aaron*, drinking the yellow wine from thin glasses. She thought of the music and of the scarlet petticoat she had worn when dancing. She opened her arms and threw back her head onto the pillows, but there was no one there to kiss her. A yearning sadness roused the sobs in her throat and sent her into despair.

The cowardly weeks drew out time in a spiteful, lingering pretence. Johanna's disease had broken out with unexpected virulence. The antidote with which the doctors tormented her was powerless against it. It lodged in every tissue, it flickered under her skin, it scratched open festering sores in the pits and hollows of her flesh, it refused to move. It paralysed her thoughts and soiled her sleep with lustful dreams, from which she started up, groaning, to recognise the dreadful, hateful reality around her. Johanna missed men. Her febrile body twitched under the torture of deprivation. Every day of burning torment, every hour increased her agony. Until she could bear it no longer. One night she made her escape from the hospital. She jumped out of the window into the garden and barefoot, with just her coat over her nightdress, she climbed over the wall and into the street.

She ran through the city, burning with unearthly, sultry anticipation. Her hair, undone, fluttered round her face, and her eyes shone. One bright, marvellous thought drove her on, filling her with happiness: she was going to find the men! Her muscles strained and her feet flew over the cobbles. The shadows of belated night owls swayed across her path, and she started at the harsh light of sudden street-lamps; she was intoxicated with a delicious, heavy, tantalising sweetness. The twin spires of the Tyn Church appeared before her, standing pale among the stars. She was as good as home! There was the street where the raucous music blared behind curtained doors, and where the women's laughter beat with its wings against the red window-panes . . .

She stopped and stared, dazzled, at the squint-eyed moon stuck against the sky which was shining down on splintered beams and rubble. The *Salon Aaron* had disappeared. Pick and shovel had demolished the house piece by piece, and the stones were stacked beside the synagogue. One single, jagged crest of masonry rose up among the ruins, and Johanna recognised her bedroom wall. Numb with horror, her eye followed the line of the street. The gaudy lights of the houses of pleasure had been extinguished, and dust rose like smoke from the blasted roofs. Everywhere ruins emerged from the darkness. While she had been wrestling with the disease in her damp bed in the hospital, they had destroyed her home.

A scream detached itself from her throat and quivered its hideous way through the deserted quarter. Her hair spilled over her coat; the night breeze blew it open and fumbled her under her nightdress. A bunch of tipsy soldiers came along. Unable to control herself, she fell to her knees before them, moaning confused words of love. And among the ruins of the demolished brothel, she gave herself to the men that chance had thrown into her path. She gave herself to them, one after the other, and her wretched body, wasted with disease, did not tire but, shuddering in the ecstasy of love, dug itself ever deeper into the rubble.

Between one summer and the next, the ghetto was torn down. New houses pressed down on the dark, unhealthy crannies, which for centuries had been the haunt of misery and vice. Clattering along on its high-heeled shoes, debauchery fled to the farthest edges of the suburbs. A city for the rich and respectable grew up over the old squares. But never in the history of Prague were the ravages of syphilis so terrible, so devastating as in that year. It invaded family life and struck the young mothers with terror. It hung on the smile of love, turning it into a leaden grin. Young boys killed themselves and old men cursed life.